WAR HORSE

Books by Fairfax Downey

DOG OF WAR

WAR HORSE

INDIAN FIGHTING ARMY

PORTRAIT OF AN ERA, AS DRAWN
BY C. D. GIBSON

RICHARD HARDING DAVIS—HIS DAY

BURTON, ARABIAN NIGHTS ADVENTURER

THE GRANDE TURKE

YOUNG ENOUGH TO KNOW BETTER

WHEN WE WERE RATHER OLDER

FATHER'S FIRST TWO YEARS

A COMIC HISTORY OF YALE

WAR HORSE

BY

FAIRFAX DOWNEY

ILLUSTRATED BY

PAUL BROWN

DODD, MEAD & COMPANY
NEW YORK   1945

Published April, 1942
Second Printing September, 1942
Third Printing December, 1942
Fourth Printing May, 1943
Fifth Printing March, 1944
Sixth Printing April, 1945

PRINTED IN THE UNITED STATES OF AMERICA
BY THE VAIL-BALLOU PRESS, INC., BINGHAMTON, N. Y.

TO THE 12TH FIELD ARTILLERY
AND TO "JEANNE D'ARC"

ACKNOWLEDGMENTS

THE author is deeply grateful to A. C. Gallagher, former
lieutenant, 12th Field Artillery, who suggested this story,
and to Howard Bloomfield, former editor of *Adventure*
where a short version appeared, for wise counsel in re-
vision; also to the late Capt. Michael V. Gannon, when
editor of *The Field Artillery Journal*, for his advice.

No writer of a horse story could fail to be proud when
his work is illustrated by Paul Brown.

For permission for verse quotations, thanks are due
John Chapman, son of my old friend, the late Arthur
Chapman; to *The Field Artillery Journal*, and to other
sources.

CONTENTS

ILLUSTRATIONS

ILLUSTRATIONS

Hast thou given the horse strength?
Hast thou clothed his neck with thunder?
Canst thou make him afraid as a grasshopper?
The glory of his nostrils is terrible.
He paweth in the valley, and rejoiceth in his strength,
He goeth on to meet the armed men.
He mocketh at fear and is not affrighted;
Neither turneth he back from the sword.
The quiver rattleth against him,
The glittering spear and the shield.
He swalloweth the ground with fierceness and rage:
Neither believeth he that it is the sound of the trumpet.
He saith among the trumpets, Ha, ha,
And he smelleth the battle afar off,
The thunder of the captains, and the shouting.

JOB XXXIX: 19–25

WAR HORSE

A tattoo on his ribs

1: THE HORSE AND THE MAN

Twenty of us ridin' bronks, headed for the war;
Twenty top-hand saddlemen, up in bustin' lore;
Off the ranges fast they come, hosses black and gray,
Hosses roan and calico, hosses brown and bay;
Saddle, bridle, cinch and ride—buck, you big hoss, buck!
You will be the captain's choice—'bye, old nag—good luck!

WAR HORSE

'Tillery and cavalry, 'tillery and cavalry,
That's the way they pick 'em when the judges are at work;
'Tillery and cavalry, 'tillery and cavalry,
Farewell, Western mountain hoss, and don't you ever shirk;
Steel and lead and powder smoke, there acrost the way—
If it wasn't I'm a neutral I'd be off with you today.

ARTHUR CHAPMAN: *The War-Horse Buyers*

MILLING masses of horses jammed the corrals of the big Kansas City Remount Depot. Under the summer sun tossing manes and shifting backs gave the effect of a broad grain field, swept by wind, a field sombre in tone. Bays mingled with blacks, sorrels, chestnuts, roans, and a few dark grays. In all that herd there was not a single white, buckskin or pinto, for these were war horses. No animal with a light-colored hide would reach France to draw the fire of German batteries.

A Texan perched on the top rail of a fence gazed out over the crowded corrals and marveled. Veteran of many a round-up though he was, Jim Thomas never had seen so many horses gathered in one place. The lot he had helped herd here was lost in this multitude. It, in turn, was only a small fraction of the cavalcade of hundreds of thousands of horses and mules North America had been shipping the Allies since 1914 and which the United States, now in 1917, was mustering for its own war effort.

A sudden commotion among the horses near him caught the Texan's attention. A big black gelding was bullying a little chestnut mare, shoving her around with his heavy shoulders, and from the look of his laid-back ears using considerable bad language.

"No way to treat a lady," muttered Jim Thomas.

He watched more closely. Why, that little mare had been in the bunch he brought up here. Several times he had singled her out and liked the looks of her. He remembered thinking that if he had found her back on his home range he would have tried her out in his string.

The mare kept moving away, but the tough black was determined to pick a fight. He arched his neck, bared his teeth and darted forward viciously to bite. Swiftly the mare sprang away, wheeled like a flash. Her dainty hoofs beat out a tattoo on the ribs of the astonished black. The bully snorted, squealed with pain and dashed away to hide himself in the herd.

"*Yippee!*" yelled Thomas. " 'Atta girl! Sock him again!"

The mare stood fast, looking up at the man on the fence. Thomas, grinning down at her, could have sworn he saw a twinkle in her eyes. Trim and small—barely fifteen hands high—she was shaggy and unkempt, not much of a horse on casual observation. But the Texan's expert inspection marked her strong shoulders and haunches, those clean legs of hers. She bore the brand of a big ranch. Perhaps originally she had been roped in one of those wild horse round-ups the vast demand nowadays was causing. As if she realized she was being admired, the mare tossed her head.

More than the light frame and wiry legs, that narrow, well-shaped head told Jim Thomas something. With renewed interest he scanned the width of forehead, sign of brains and courage—the soft eyes, capable of sparkling with excitement—the small, alert ears—wide nostrils which would flare at a gallop and show scarlet as fire.

"Arab blood, sure enough, and more'n a little," he said under his breath.

He was right. Out of the deserts of Arabia had come the mare's fleet forebears to carry the fierce squadrons of Islam on their path of conquest through Egypt and High Barbary and Spain; to become the spoils of war when King Ferdinand thrust the Saracens out of their last strongholds in Granada; to make the fearsome voyage to the New World in frail caravels and be ridden roughshod by the Spaniards over the Empire of Montezuma, whose Aztec warriors fled in greater terror of the strange, snorting beasts than of the lances and flashing swords of their riders; to win from their masters, the Conquistadores, the tribute set down in their chronicles: "For, after God, we owed the victory to our horses."

Such was the mare's distinguished ancestry. Yet every other American horse also stemmed back to those steeds, bred in the settlements of New Spain or multiplying on the plains where stray animals gathered in wild herds. The chestnut mare was remarkable in that the tricks of heredity had endowed her with a stronger strain from that ancient lineage.

"You're real folks, little lady," the Texan decided. "*Saludes, caballo!*" And he swept off his hat in tribute.

The mare leaped nervously away at the gesture, galloping to the far side of the corral.

"Sorry," the man called after her. "Reckon some broncho buster's been fanning you plenty. Don't blame you for not trusting any man."

Well, that was that. Let her go. Some clodhopping soldier would be getting a better mount than he knew and probably ruin her entirely—which was none of Jim Thomas's affair. He stared lazily across the corral to where a group of cowboys had gathered. From the laughing and yelling, they had been making the rounds of Kansas City saloons. One long, lanky puncher climbed through the rails of the fence with a lariat, loosened its coils and whirled it. As the horses near him scattered, he threw. The loop settled over the neck of the little chestnut mare and was drawn taut.

The mare stood. She knew the rope of old. Swaggering over, the tall puncher quickly took two turns of the rope around the mare's nose and vaulted onto her back. Long legs wrapped around her. The spectacle of the big man on the little horse struck the cowboy's companions as outrageously funny.

To Jim Thomas, watching with a frown, it seemed a downright indignity.

Swish! Whack! A quirt raised dust on the mare's hide. For an instant of quivering surprise, she did not move. Then she lit out. She pitched, mixing high jumps with low. She varied her rhythm. Only such a fine rider as the tall man was could have stuck on bareback.

"Go it, Shorty!" "Get some glue on your pants!" The rider's outfit cheered him wildly from the fence. But the mare had had enough of this insulting procedure. Directly in front of the gallery, she slid to a stop with stiff legs and suddenly whirled, swapping ends. The lanky puncher hit the dust with a thud.

Amid cheers from the bunch, he got to his feet. Then he did something he might never have done if he had not been a little drunk and his pride hurt.

He still held an end of his rope. Rapidly he snubbed it around a fence post and, running along to where the mare strained against it, grabbed her by the mane and began kicking her in the belly.

The next thing he knew, he kicked air and sat down hard. A stranger stood over him closing the jackknife that had severed the lariat. There was a steely glint in the gray eyes that glared down on him. Close-compressed lips over a squared jaw opened.

"Any *hombre*," said Jim Thomas, "that'll kick a horse is a—"

Paul Brown

He took one on the chin

The Texan made it emphatic and specific. By the time he had finished, the tall puncher was up and at him with flailing fists. Knuckles smacked on flesh. Dust from scuffling feet enveloped the fighters. Thomas backed away from his adversary, sparing a glance over his shoulder, half expecting some of Shorty's friends to pile onto him from behind. No, it was to be fair play. Most of the gallery, ashamed of the kicking, were yelling for the stranger.

Shorty, towering over the Texan and outreaching him by three inches, landed a couple of jolting punches. Jim spat blood and closed in. He swung hard, missed and took more punishment. Doggedly he bored in again. Right and left, he smashed at the other's stomach.

"How's it feel in *your* belly?" he demanded and hit again.

The tall man grunted, "*Woof!*" His guard dropped, and he took one on the chin. For the third time he imprinted a beautiful impression of his posterior in the dirt of the corral.

"Got enough," he gasped, sitting there.

The cowboys crowded around Jim Thomas, slapping his back.

"Good scrap, fella!" one of them said. "But look yonder."

The horses in the corral were being herded toward a chute, to pass before the Government buyers. Among them the little chestnut mare, the loop of the lariat still around her neck, walked quietly.

"Stranger," the cowboy grinned at Jim Thomas, "there goes the lady friend yuh fit for. And she didn't even thank yuh!"

Beside a veterinary stood a captain of the Remount Service. Dapper in his well-cut boots with the tone of old mahogany, the captain might have been put down as an Eastern tenderfoot, masquerading as a judge of horse-flesh, by those who did not know him as a noted Master of Fox Hounds and owner of a private racing stable. He was one of the fifty best-known horsemen in the United States, who had been commissioned captains in the Reserve Corps and assigned to the purchase boards of the Remount Service. They would make an altogether remarkable record, with few complaints on their vast number of selections.

"What's the verdict, Doctor?" asked the captain, cocking a quizzical eye at the mare.

"Small, no mere filly, but sound as a dollar," answered the veterinary.

"*Humph*," said the captain. "Bet she can jump. By Nimrod, the son of Kush, bet I could make that little mare into 'a mighty hunter before the Lord!' "

Conscious of a scrutiny, the captain glanced up at the compact figure sitting on the fence, a figure a little above medium height, shoulders a trifle stooped from long hours in the saddle. The sun-bronzed features, shadowed by a faded ten-gallon hat, were grave; the mouth firm, as of one habitually taciturn. Under those worn chaps, the legs probably were bowed. A typical cowboy, the captain decided. He met an interested gaze in the clear, gray eyes of Jim Thomas, who had followed the mare to the inspection chute, unable to refrain from seeing what happened to her.

"Yep, bet she can jump," the officer said again. "What do you think, cowboy?"

"Reckon she can, Cap," was the answer. "She's got something."

"Right you are," the captain agreed. He scanned the mare's points. "Right you are," he repeated. "What she's got, somehow or t'other, is Arab blood in good measure."

"Passed for Uncle Sam," the officer decreed and waved the mare on. Half serious, half jesting, he spoke to the man on the fence.

"Go round up some Germans on her, cowboy," he said.

So somehow the Texan, his ranch outfit left behind, had found himself in the box car with the mare as one of the shipment escort. Just what the impulse was he never quite recognized. Was it the Remount captain's words? Or was it a vague feeling that he ought to see if the mare landed in good hands? He couldn't quite decide. Where he went didn't matter much, just so he was working with horses.

It was a slow trip East, with the train shunted often onto sidings, but the horses kept it from being a dull one for Thomas. What fine, strong, intelligent fellows they were, patiently munching hay in the car racks. Averaging from fifteen hands two inches to a hand taller, weighing about 1200 pounds, they were an ideal field artillery type. Many of them were draft animals from farms, for the day of the tractor had not yet dawned; and some of the best of these were three-year-olds, by Government-owned stallions out of farm mares, bred and sold under contract to the Remount at $150 a head. Out of them, the Army, which would spend a total of sixty-two million dollars on war horses and mules, got more than its money's worth.

Mingled with the draft horses were lighter animals like the chestnut mare, mounts for officers, noncoms, and details. These might have served for cavalry, but the regiments of that gallant arm, doomed by the deadly machine gun, were dwindling, being converted into artillery.

The mare stood with legs braced against the swaying box car. Every other horse in the car, packed flank to flank and facing opposite directions, loomed over her. Had it been possible for her to be jostled by her heavier companions, she might have slipped and fallen, a slender leg snapping. Then a merciful pistol bullet would have crashed between her eyes, and the journey of one more war horse, bound for battle overseas, would have ended at some watering stop in Illinois or Ohio.

But Jim Thomas had taken precautions against just such an accident. He had rigged up a stall for the mare next his own quarters at an end of the car. There she rode in comparative safety, and when the sunburned young Texan was kidded by the train crew and asked if he were taking that runt of a mare to General Pershing, he only grinned.

In spite of all his care, the mare regarded him with distrust. That, he knew, was the result of bad treatment she must have had. It could not be otherwise with an intelligent horse of good blood. Perhaps time and kindness would cure her, perhaps not. The man sensed that, beneath her suspicion, there was real companionship in the little mare. She had the endearing qualities of other horses he had known and grown fond of in a life spent mostly in the saddle—the little pinto which had been his during boyhood on his father's ranch; the claybank on which he had ridden the range for two seasons; that polo pony he had helped train in California; the Kentucky colt which had become a famous steeplechaser. As the others used to do, Thomas once or twice caught the chestnut following him with big, soft eyes. Between them might grow that bond of devotion and loyalty which sometimes binds man, the master, and his servants, the horse and the dog. The elephant, they say, knows that tie also, and sometimes the more independent, self-sufficient cat.

Jim Thomas was well aware that it was all sentimental

folly. Always he had been a wanderer, restless and foot-loose. It never did to become too attached to a horse. It tied a man down more or less. With this mare, it must be as it had been with the others. The train was chuffing over the Alleghenies now. Before long they would be in Washington. Then they would turn the horses over to the Army, and that would be the last Jim Thomas saw of any of them.

Another day and a night and they pulled into Washington yards. The travel-weary horses were led from the cars, kicking and skittish, plainly overjoyed to be on firm ground again. A harassed officer marshaled his scant horse detail. Thomas hesitated. Then, "Need any help?" he offered.

"Sure do," the officer answered. "Got to get these nags all the way to Fort Myer. More of 'em than I counted on. Much obliged if you'll lend a hand. Saddle up."

Would he ride the mare? Why not? He'd never see her again and this was his last chance. Tempted though he was, Jim Thomas saddled a bay instead. The little chestnut, he thought, had begun to know him a little, to consider with that keen perception many horses have that he might be a friend. If he mounted her now, it might come to a struggle for mastery; and there was a slower but a better way. So the mare was one of the two led horses with which he joined the column clattering through the city streets. Admiringly he noted how smooth-gaited and sure-footed she was on the unaccustomed asphalt.

Washington felt like a war—much more than the West had. There was no doubt about the atmosphere when the column, having crossed the bridge into Virginia, climbed the hill to Fort Myer. The parade ground yonder was covered with khaki battalions, rank on rank. A bugle call, "Retreat," floated clear and sweet through the afternoon air. "Halt," called the officer, and Thomas reined in the bay. The bugle ceased, the officer ordered, "Detail, 'tenshun." A band played *The Star-Spangled Banner*, the sunset gun putting a period to its last stirring chord. All along the column, the green horses shied and jumped. The line moved on to the corrals. Thomas turned in the mare with the rest.

The officer was beside him, speaking. "Thanks a lot. You helped me out of a hole. I'll see you get chow and a bunk in the barracks for the night. You've got transportation back West?"

"Sure have. All set, thanks."

"Not in the Service, are you?" the other continued. "We can use you Westerners that know how to handle horses."

"Reckon I may get in some day."

"Fair enough." The officer called over a corporal. "Take care of this man in the mess and see that he gets a bunk." He turned to go.

"Lieutenant," Thomas called after him, "where's this

lot of horses bound?"

"They're filling out the quota of a new artillery regiment in camp about ten miles from here. Well, so long and thanks again."

Thoughtfully Jim Thomas followed the corporal. No great hurry about getting back West. He'd kind of like to see what happened. It would be a shame if they let some clumsy, heavy galoot ride that little mare.

Charge!

2: THE STABLE SERGEANT'S CHOICE

Who is he that may water the horse and not drink himself?
ANON. *Old English Homilies*

THE matter of the mare's future was decided that very night by two bottles of liquid lightning, fifty loose mules, and one black eye.

On pass from the Virginia encampment where a brand-new field artillery outfit was being raised to be a soldier, Stable Sergeant Michael Quinn of Battery D marched upon the venerable town of Alexandria. In a tavern, he sighted the aforementioned two bottles as a target, bracketed them and passed rapidly into fire for effect. There was no question of the effect when he ceased firing and started back for camp with just time enough to make it before the midnight limit. By bluff, blarney, and the strength of his chevrons, he got past the guard. Elated, expansive, he swung along with an On-to-Berlin air. Jubilantly he began to sing the regimental song.

We don't know where we're going, but we're on our way.
We're out to make a showing for the —th F.A.
And when the Kaiser sees us, you will hear him say,
"I don't know where I'm going but I'm on my way."

So chanted Sergeant Michael Quinn and strode onward. Nothing could stop him, no, nothing—

In the darkness dead ahead of him a bell tolled a single, sepulchral note. A long, white, ghostly visage thrust itself straight at him. The sergeant gasped and staggered back, too frozen to run. The ghostly visage nodded benevolently. With a long sigh of relief, Sergeant Quinn recognized the apparition—the old, blaze-faced bell mare. She had broken loose from the Supply Company's picket line yonder, where her loyal following of mules, hearing her bell and missing her, stamped and snorted.

"You old darlint, throwin' a scare inter me like that!" he chided, embracing the gentle animal. Good cheer flooded back over him. "Prepare to mount. Mount," he commanded himself, and hoisted himself up on her back. "Forward, ho!" ordered Stable Sergeant Quinn, and off he rode, the bell at the mare's neck clanking loudly.

All along the picket line, long ears waggled and pricked up at the familiar summons. Straining at their tie ropes, the mules attempted to demonstrate that marvelous discovery made by some benefactor of the human race: that those stubborn, balky hybrids, which so often refuse the leadership of mere man, will follow a bell mare anywhere. As the sound of the bell receded, some fifty mules slipped headstalls or broke ropes and trotted after their guiding star.

Sergeant Quinn glanced back and grinned with vast satisfaction. "Forward, ye jugheads!" he shouted. "Trot! Gallop!"

Through the tent-lined battery streets raced the cavalcade, bell clanging, hoofs thundering, ears flapping. Canvas collapsed on sleeping artillerymen, as guy ropes were snapped in the stampede. Every sentry on post clamored for the corporal of the guard. Animals from other picket lines wrenched loose and joined the hurly-burly. Officers' Row erupted frantic figures, attired in tunics, pajama pants, and automatic pistols, buckled on for a last stand against the foe or whatever the tremendous racket was. The bugler of the guard blew a series of discordant blasts which sounded like a combination of the *Call to Arms* and *The Darktown Strutters' Ball*.

On galloped the reprehensible Sergeant Quinn, whooping and digging his heels into his mount's flanks, finally to bring up in mid-career smack against the side of a mess hall. It was Second Lieutenant John Brent of his own battery who cornered the wild cavalier there and turned a flashlight on him.

"Get off that horse, Sergeant!" he ordered, grabbing the headstall.

"Lay off!" Quinn roared. "Leggo! Don't know where I'm going but I'm on me way!"

Brent tugged at his leg. Whereupon the sergeant leaned over and clouted his would-be captor in his eye.

The next instant he was swept from his steed and was being shaken into sobriety in the grasp of big First Sergeant McNally.

"You fool you, Quinn! You drunken fool! Striking an officer!" McNally groaned. "You done enough hitches in this here Army to know what that means. Leavenworth and hard labor, you fool!"

He turned to Brent sadly. "Sir, the lieutenant will have to prefer charges. I'm witness."

Brent, rubbing his eye, shook his head in denial. A green, young officer but wise beyond his years or his length of service. "No," he refused. "I'll not prefer charges. Quinn is drunk and didn't know what he was doing. Besides, he's too good a stable sergeant to lose. Nobody saw it but us. If this eye of mine turns into a shiner, I'll blame it on a mule. It felt like one anyway."

In the frosty, blue eyes of the veteran McNally shone a gleam of admiration. There might still be a chance of winning a war with a bunch of civilians in uniform, if there were enough of them like this lad. "Very good, sir," he said and led away the bell mare.

"Get to your quarters and sleep it off, Sergeant Quinn," Brent directed. "Tomorrow you've got to pick the best of that new draft of horses for Battery D."

The leader of the charge of the mule brigade saluted uncertainly and weaved away.

Stable Sergeant Quinn, pale and bleary-eyed, was on hand the next noon when the horses sent over from Fort Myer were brought into camp and picketed. On the surface they looked an unpromising lot, shoeless, hides caked with dirt, tousle-maned, tails almost dragging on the ground. A few officers and the old noncoms who had been the nucleus of the new regiment, knew better. A smile of approval pushed up the military mustache of the regiment's commander. Colonel Mack knew good artillery motive power when he saw it and had known it since those days, seventeen years ago, when, as a young lieutenant, he rode with Reilly's Battery to the relief of the Legations in Pekin.

The battery commanders drew for order of choice of horses, but their crafty old stable sergeants did the actual picking. Here one veteran chose an agile lead horse. There another indicated a strong wheel horse, complaining bitterly when a likely mate for it was snapped up by the next chooser. Selection went on slowly, rivalry hot.

Jim Thomas, hovering solicitously around the chestnut mare, heard a fierce whisper at his elbow.

"Whist! And who might you be?" Sergeant Quinn of D Battery was glaring at him.

"Me? Oh, I helped bring these horses East."

"I'll thank you to quit pointing that little chestnut mare like one iv thim hunting dawgs."

"All right. But I'm sort of interested in her."

"So will the likes iv thim ither sergeants be if you kape on passing her in review under their eyes. Lay off till my turn comes 'round agin."

"I'll do that." Thomas turned his back on the mare. "Know a good horse when you see one, don't you, Sarge?"

Quinn crooked a thumb at the khaki horse head on his chevrons. "Sure and did you think that was a goat?" he growled.

"Battery D's choice," announced the sergeant-major.

Quinn strolled all along the line. "Tough pickings by this time," he said. Finally he nonchalantly indicated the chestnut. "I'll be taking this here gazelle," he declared. "Lead out, orderly."

"Who'll be riding the little mare?" Thomas asked.

"Why? What of it?"

"Nothin' special. Just wondered."

"Know something about the nag, don't yuh? Come on, spill it."

"Well, I saw a little of her out at the depot in Kaysee, and I brought her East. She's got the makings, but she's had rotten treatment somewheres before she was bought. If she's handled right, she'll make a grand *caballo*. If she ain't, she'll turn mean or end up a broken-spirited plug after some bum beats the hide off her."

It was a long speech for the Texan. He took a breath and resumed: "It'll take time and patience for somebody that knows horses. Reckon you could do it, Sarge."

"Not me, m' boy. I'm nurse to two hundred iv thim animules in the batt'ry. No time for private patients."

"Who'll be riding her?" Thomas persisted.

Sergeant Quinn's jovial Irish eyes turned crafty. "Oh, I dunno. Some officer mebbe. Mebbe that young looten-ant there." He waved a hand toward Lieutenant Brent cutting across the parade ground.

"Him with the eye in deep mourning?"

"That's him."

"Somebody who packed a real wallop hung that shanty on him."

"Do you say so now?" Quinn replied with an air of gratification. "They do claim it was a mule done it."

"Can he ride?"

"He sticks on by the grace o' God."

"He don't know horses then."

"Well, he's met some, formal."

Thomas contemptuously marked the officer's brand new boots. "He'd wreck the little mare," he declared bitterly.

"Well, he don't get her if I don't tell him she's a good horse. Now if I had some good man who'd really take her in hand—"

The old reprobate paused. He had every intention of giving the mare to Lieutenant Brent in return for his forebearance of the previous night. Yet he realized from what this civilian had told him that she must be gentled and put into shape first.

"Sure an' if I had somebody to take her in hand and train her," he repeated, " 'twould be only right he'd be the lad to have her for his mount."

Jim Thomas was silent as they walked into the Battery D area. Quinn let him ferment. At the picket line, the Stable Sergeant spoke:

"Well, here's the battery picket line. It's back West you'll be going now, so say good-by to your friend there."

Jim Thomas walked over toward the little mare. Recognizing him, she nickered. Nobody seemed to be looking.

He put an arm around her neck and spoke into a velvety ear.

"Good-by, old girl," he whispered. "Good luck to you over there."

He turned hurriedly and strode away.

One glance back. Ah, that was a mistake. The mare, curving her graceful neck as far as the picket rope allowed, was looking after him reproachfully with her great, dark eyes.

A voice sounded behind him. "Whist, lad," Stable Sergeant Quinn hailed him, looking away and pretending not to have seen the moisture in the Texan's eyes. "To whom it may be concerning, there's a recruiting station over to Fort Myer. It might be somebody would be wanting to jine up. 'Twould be no trick at all to get assigned to this rigimint. And, come to think iv it, I'm after needing a stable orderly."

Thomas dug the toe of a boot into the ground. Crazy idea, that, getting into a foreigners' war. He didn't have to go—not till there was a draft anyway. Only professional soldiers and volunteers were going now—they and a lot of poor horses that couldn't help themselves.

"Hang it!" he muttered under his breath. Then, moving away, he called back, "Thanks, Sarge. So long. Reckon I might be seeing you again."

Even the well-oiled conscience of Sergeant Quinn suffered a twinge at that. No buck private would be getting the mare—not when Mike Quinn could pay a past favor with her and lay up credit for future ones.

"It's a dirty trick I've been after playing on the lad," he muttered to himself. "But sure he oughter be in the Army anyways. An' it's no more iv a lie I've told him than thim recruitin' sergeants does."

Swept across the battery front.

3: THE MARE WINS A NAME

Young Jim—he packed the red guidon
  In the pipin' times o' peace.
Say, the kid could ride when he changed the guide
  Like a streak o' lightnin' grease!

With the batt'ry rumblin' on behind,
  Up the B.C.'s arm ud go,—
Jim's sorrel mare you can bet knew where
  To dust when the bugles blow.
She cut across the batt'ry front,
  Teams gallopin' like ez not,
An' Jim sits tight an' the guide is right,
  In the crack uv a pistol shot.

FAIRFAX DOWNEY: *The Guidon Bearer*

CINDERELLA, dressing for the ball, was not more hand-somely arrayed than the chestnut mare, nor was the former lady's transformation more startling. Neatly shod, mane and tail trimmed and brushed, coat groomed to shine like satin, the mare tossed her head and seemed to take a feminine pride in her own appearance. Her hand maidens, two sweating buck privates, finally were relieved of the duty. Theirs had been no easy task, for the mare was hard to handle.

Sergeant Quinn started in search of Second Lieutenant John Brent. He found him in the gun park and saluted with military precision. "Sor, Stable Sergeant Quinn requests permission to speak to the Lootenant."

"Say on, Sergeant," granted Brent, grinning.

"Sor, fresh in me mimory is the unfortynate ruckus a night or so ago. But for the lootenant, I'd be fighting the war on a rock pile at Leavenworth. The luck iv the Irish is no liss than their gratitood. I've got a good mount for the lootenant down on the picket line, if he'll come look."

"Anything but a mule," said Johnny Brent, faintly winking his black eye. "They kick like thunder."

Down on the line, Quinn displayed the mare with the air of a proud parent with his first-born.

"She's a beauty," Brent responded. "But—but isn't she pretty small, Sergeant?"

For what Johnny Brent, romantic chap, wanted was a mighty charger. Too much reading of days when knighthood was in flower had done that to him. Of course, war was different now. Only tanks were armored. While the German Uhlans, he had heard, still carried lances, they seemed disinclined to chivalry. As for artillery officers, they had been deprived even of swords, good blades to carve the casques of men. Still at least, one could ride, booted and spurred, into the fray upon a tall steed that spurned the earth and snorted with the lust of battle.

"Small, sor?" Sergeant Quinn broke in on his musings. "Sure and she's no gi-raffe. But I'm telling the lootenant she's the best mount in the regiment."

"Nobody'd know better than you, Sergeant."

"I'll not deny it, sor, and it's something we'd better be kaping dark. Wance 'tis known, the lootenant'll be ranked out iv her. We'll be letting the ither officers pick their mounts first. Besides, the mare ain't ready for the lootenant yit. She's being trained by a Texas lad—only a rookie but he knows horses."

Mike Quinn had taken good care Jim Thomas should

be far from the picket line at this moment and never suspect his perfidy.

"So not a word to nobody," continued Quinn, "not even to the Texas lad. In a few weeks she'll be the lootenant's and he'll be having a prize."

Brent was convinced. "Thanks a lot, Sergeant," he said. "I'll not forget the favor."

The training of the mare was conducted with infinite gentleness and patience by the unsuspecting Jim Thomas. Well aware that her previous education had been a rough and ready affair, he treated her much as he would a green horse. Often he fed her by hand with wisps of hay or grass. He never made any sudden movement near her. For every lesson she learned he rewarded her with food. While Quinn watched with professional admiration, the Texan grasped a lock of the mare's mane with one hand and ran the other slowly down a leg until she was ready to allow him to raise and clean her hoofs. She lost her head-shyness because he was careful not to force the bit into her mouth and not to hurt her ears when he drew the bridle over them. In chill weather he warmed the bit with his hands and it was always bright and clean, a fact which the dainty creature seemed to appreciate. He leaned on her back with his elbow and patted her neck before he ventured to mount. When it was time to saddle up, he put blanket and saddle on and off repeatedly until she became accustomed to them and no longer jerked away, and his cinching was a masterpiece of deliberation.

Naturally docile, the mare responded rapidly to his understanding. Before long Quinn, with no misgivings whatever, sent Thomas out to ride her with the battery. Thomas's pride in the little chestnut and his affection for her grew. Tirelessly she carried him through the long, hardening marches the batteries took to teach drivers and horses their jobs. She graduated to mounted drill where, fast and handy, she could "wheel on a dime" like a polo pony. Often Thomas noticed Lieutenant Brent watching the mare admiringly. Perhaps, the Texan reflected, that young officer wasn't such a greenhorn after all. If he could see the mare's points, there was hope for him.

For his part, Johnny Brent longed for the day when the mare would be his. The mount he was riding was heavy-gaited and inclined to stumble. The confounded nag might fall with him in front of a galloping battery some day; vividly imagining it, Brent could almost feel the iron wheels of the carriages making a rut through his chest. Now on the sure-footed little mare a man could ride gloriously.

He was beginning to feel the dash and *élan* of the Field Artillery, modern though it was. Guns and caissons thundering along in clouds of dust like the smoke of battle. The red guidon with its golden crossed cannon, a veritable oriflamme, snapping in the wind. The battery commander's outflung fist, the blare of a bugle, shrill whistle blasts, and shouts of "Action front!" Teams wheeling about and pulled to a halt with a rattle of single-trees and toggle chains. Cannoneers jumping from the carriages, unlimbering, preparing for action. Horses and limbers galloping to the rear. A string of commands and swift activity behind the gun shields. "Fire!" The roar of a volley, and yonder, over the distant targets, the white puffs of bursting shrapnel.

So it happened that Johnny Brent no longer regretted that mêlées of mailed knights were things of the past. He now read drill regs, treatises on conduct of fire, and tales of artillery and artillerymen of his own land—of staunch old Henry Knox, Washington's chief of artillery, and of certain of his young battery commanders who did well after the war, too, in Government jobs—chaps named Madison and Monroe and Alexander Hamilton —of Sergeant Molly Pitcher who manned her fallen husband's gun at Monmouth—of O'Brien and his Bulldogs, the bronze muzzle-loading cannon that raked Mexican battlefields from Buena Vista to Chapultepec;—of gallant Cushing and Hunt, who wore the blue in '61, and the dashing gray horse artillery of Pellham and Pegram —of Capron's Battery in the Indian wars, of Grimes' in Cuba and Reilly's in China, and others on that stirring roll.

Behind the artillery lay history: ancient, honorable and fascinating. Why, it was the artillery, Brent read, that invented the cigarette. When an Egyptian gun squad at the siege of Acre lost the only pipe it possessed in a shell explosion, one of the cannoneers, eager for a smoke, had taken a spill (the twist of paper used to wrap a powder train), filled it with tobacco and lit up.

In the olden times the great cannon were duly christened and handsomely embossed with the names of any of the Twelve Apostles—always excepting Judas, which in view of the cannons' treacherous propensity to burst, would have been tempting fate. And one day Brent learned from one of the older officers that the artillery boasted a patron saint of its own.

Full of the discovery, he hurried down to the picket line. The chestnut mare was contentedly receiving a thorough grooming from that Texas lad who had been training her. Sergeant Quinn, standing near by, saluted.

"Got a name for the mare at last, Sergeant," Brent announced enthusiastically.

Quinn made frantic motions for silence, pointing toward Thomas. The Texan must not be allowed yet to catch on to the trick being played on him. But the lieutenant, eyes on the mare, failed to notice. Quinn began talking fast to cover up.

"A name? Fine, sor. Ivery horse in the battery had oughter be christened. Don't know how we forgot this here one."

"The mare deserves a good one," Brent hurried on.

"And I've got it. We'll call her Santa Barbara."

"After that there town in California, sor?" asked Quinn, still making unseen grimaces.

"No, after the original of the name. Beautiful maiden named Barbara who got to be a saint. What's more, the patron saint of the artillery."

"There's times, sor," the stable sergeant put in, "when the artillery could do with a saint."

"I don't doubt it," Brent laughed. "But listen to the story of Santa Barbara. She lived 'way back in the old days. Had an ornery old heathen for a father. He shut her up in a tower. Didn't want her either to get married or get religion. But in spite of him, a missionary in disguise got into the tower and converted Barbara to Christianity."

"*Dominus vobiscum*," declared Sergeant Quinn unexpectedly.

"Same to you, Sergeant," said Lieutenant Brent. "But her father found out and got good and sore. He had the poor girl beaten and tortured. The gentle Barbara endured it all with courage and would not give up her faith. Then her father drove her out to the top of a mountain, drew his sword and with his own hands struck off her head!"

"Why," Sergeant Quinn broke in, "the old divvil! The old—"

"All of that, Sergeant. But the fair Barbara, martyred, became a saint."

"Rest her sowl," murmured Sergeant Quinn.

"Amen," responded the lieutenant. "But that's not all the story. When the old man started down the mountain, black clouds gathered and a storm broke. It thundered like a rolling barrage. Then, as a poet puts it:

'The dread artillery of Heaven flashed.'

A bolt of lightning streaked down!"

"Hooray!" roared Sergeant Quinn. "Got the old—"

"Right. Got him. A direct hit. The old heathen dropped in his tracks. So that was how Barbara became the patron saint of the artillery."

Lieutenant Brent observed with some pleasure that he had held his audience. He looked at the sunburned recruit by the mare's side and said, "Santa Barbara. Think it's a good name for the mare, soldier?"

"Maybe Barbara for short, sir."

"Sure."

"It's a good name," the Texan decided. "The mare's kinda like that—like that girl you told about. There's real stuff in her. Reckon you could count on her when the time came."

"*Hmm*," murmured Brent. "You could, I'm sure. Barbara it is then."

He was feeling a little disturbed about this business. It would be kind of tough on this nice lad to lose the mare.

Still, Thomas must realize that, as a private, he couldn't expect to keep as fine a mount as Barbara. It would be decent, though, to show appreciation of the way the mare had been trained.

Brent said, "By the way, the Captain's on the sick list and wants me to exercise his horse. I'm taking drill this afternoon. Guidon bearer's sick, too. Thomas, if Sergeant Quinn can teach you your post and how to change the guide, you can carry the stick today and ride the mare. You've done wonders with her."

"Thanks, sir," the Texan answered as the lieutenant walked away. He started brushing Barbara, his brows knit. "Say, Sarge," he broke out. "Looks like that officer's got his eye on the mare. Now look here. She's mine. No shave-tail's going to—"

"Horsefeathers, m' boy," deprecated the guileful Quinn. A smile of bland and beautiful reassurance wreathed his features. "Did he make any move to take her over? Didn't you hear him tell you to ride her this aft?"

"Yep. Reckon I was wrong. Sorry, Sarge," Thomas apologized.

Drill went well that afternoon. The battery, pretty well shaken down, swung handily from column of sections into line. It took up a trot and, obeying Lieutenant Brent's pointed finger, the guidon bearer swept across the battery front from right to left flank. The mare at a dead gallop

At a difficult angle, the mare
soared over.

was grace and rhythm personified and Jim Thomas sat his saddle as if he grew there.

"Countermarch" came the order, still at a trot. The sections turned about handsomely, executing the difficult maneuver.

"Right wheel, ho!" Brent shouted, with a horizontal sweep of his arm, and the section chiefs echoed him. The left of the line, where the red guidon streamed, broke into the gallop. Around, in a great arc, swept the long front of teams and gun carriages, pivoting on the right. But at that pace the interval between sections quickly widened, and the front expanded. Too late Brent saw that the left flank would swing too close for comfort to a fence at the edge of the field. The clatter drowned the blasts of his whistle, and dust hid his arm signals. Down on the fence dashed the outer teams, bearing right sharply now, horses and drivers leaning inward at a sharp angle. Helpless, raging at the folly of the risk he had taken, Brent could only watch.

In those few seconds he estimated that the outmost section would manage the turn just inside the fence. But never the guidon bearer. Nothing could slip through that narrow space remaining. Horse and rider were doomed to be crushed between the gun team and the fence.

In or out of action, a certain number of fatal accidents occur in the field artillery, some avoidable, some inevitable. A girth slips or a harness strap, not properly cleaned and oiled, snaps, or a cannoneer is jolted from his seat on a limber. For the men prone on the ground, the heavy carriages following are cars of the Juggernaut. A defective shell or some obstruction in the gun barrel causes a muzzle burst, and the gun squad lie mangled around the shattered piece. But this evolution Lieutenant Brent had ordered was a grandstand play, a drill hall maneuver for a veteran outfit. Too late he realized he never should have tried it at a gallop, that his guide should have been at the pivotal flank. Far from the front, he had sent a good man and a good horse to a needless, inglorious death. He tried to shut his eyes and could not.

He saw the red guidon fluttering above the dust cloud as if in farewell. Then it swung sharply outward, leaped upward. Beneath it appeared a glimpse of olive drab uniform and chestnut hide. At a difficult angle, the mare soared over that three-rail fence like a bird. On the other side, Thomas wheeled her, put her at the fence again, cleared it and galloped back to his post.

"Santa Barbara!" gasped Lieutenant Brent. It sounded like a prayer. "Walk! Halt!"

"*Yoicks!*" cried the junior lieutenant. "Likewise tally-ho! All this outfit needs is a pack of hounds and a nice Teutonic fox. Man, you mighty near expended one guidon bearer and mount."

Brent soberly led the battery back to camp. He glanced

over his shoulder once at the column where, to the left of the chief of the first section, Thomas proudly grasped the guidon and Barbara's reins. Brent's lips moved and he murmured to himself:

> She was iron-sinew'd and satin-skinn'd,
> Ribb'd like a drum and limb'd like a deer,
> Fierce as the fire and fleet as the wind—
> There was nothing she couldn't climb or clear.

Brent stayed on the line after grooming to beg Jim Thomas's pardon for the rash order that had risked his life and the mare's. No hard feelings, Thomas told him; it had come out all right. The two men, standing there together and beaming at Barbara, liked and understood each other. This might be the best time, Brent thought, to break the news.

"Thomas," he hesitated, "you've probably expected— Sergeant Quinn must have given you an idea— You see, he picked out Barbara for me. You've done a grand job training her and I sure appreciate it. Even though I'm taking her for my mount, I'll be wanting you to take care of her and ride her often."

The gray eyes of the Texan had turned hard. "Quinn —picked her for you?" he jerked out. "Why, the dirty—"

"That's enough, Private Thomas!" The young officer was up on his dignity. "You surely didn't expect to keep as good a horse as this for yourself—you a buck private. If I didn't take her, some other officer would. You're in the Army now."

Barbara turned her head and regarded the two men in a puzzled fashion. They looked at her, then glared back at each other. Jim Thomas clamped his firm mouth shut. Brent, red-faced, strode away.

Stable Sergeant Michael Quinn looked up to see a menacing figure standing in the door of his tent.

"You dirty, double-crossing liar, you!" shouted Jim Thomas.

"Aisy now," Quinn soothed. "Thim's hard words."

"Brent's taken my horse." The Texan's voice was dangerously quiet now. "You planned it all along. You knew I was keen about that little mare and was going to get fonder of her. You got me into this blasted Army by a lousy, low-down trick!"

"Sure and it was time you was in the Army anyhow."

"It was, was it? Thought I ought to be doing some fighting, did you? Well, if you weren't an older man—"

"So it's that way, m' lad," the sergeant growled. " 'Twas niver yit said iv the Irish that a bit of age ended their liking for a bit iv an argymint. I'm shedding my chevrons, see." He stripped off his shirt. "Jist step on over back iv the picket line."

Sergeant Michael Quinn was sporting a couple of beau-

tiful black eyes that evening. His story was that while looking through the bottoms of a couple of bottles, he had
been treacherously attacked by a pair of large pink ele-
phants.

Private Jim Thomas, relieved as stable orderly, was beginning a long tour of duty as kitchen police in grim
silence.

Danced to the music of the bugles.

4: OFFICERS' CALL

If you ride a horse, sit close and tight.
If you ride a man, sit easy and light.
                    FRANKLIN: *Poor Richard*

IN other camps, field artillery regiments were drilling on mock guns: stovepipes mounted on cart wheels. They even lacked horses, so tremendous had been the demand from the Allies, and they were using oversize sawhorses in attempts to teach recruits a little of sitting a saddle and harnessing. It was the old, old story of the United States entering a war, unready, ill-equipped.

Not so for the regiment in the Virginia encampment. It was destined to form part of a Regular division, elements of which already were in France, and it rejoiced in its full complement of twenty-four 3-inch guns, with accompanying caissons, limbers, supply wagons, and fire-control instruments, eked out of the scanty Government stores, as well as all the multitude of spare parts and other articles required by the tables of organization. It was blessed with all the thousand or so horses and mules a field artillery regiment at war strength should have, and they were splendid animals.

The fall of 1917 waned into the winter. Anxiety grew in the city of Washington near by. Neither news from overseas nor visible evidence indicated that America was doing much more in this war than mark time. Secretary Bryan had declared that a million men would spring to arms overnight. The men would spring—or be drafted—but production of the arms was another matter. While plenty of uniforms, worn by officers on staff duty, were apparent in Washington, there was little evidence of armed activity. It seemed high time the nation's capital was shown at least some troops marching as to war.

Therefore on a bright, frosty morning, furbished and polished to a faretheewell, the —th Field Artillery stood to horse. The bugles sang, and mounted men swung into saddles and cannoneers to carriage seats. Along the Virginia roads and over the District of Columbia line the long column rolled.

Well inside the city limits a halt was called. The band, which was not mounted, to Colonel Mack's intense regret, clambered out of trucks and formed up in the van. Every vehicle was rubbed with cloths, and horses were groomed anew. While Lieutenant Brent was inspecting his platoon, his striker jumped from his seat on a wagon to brush Barbara's mane and tail and shine her hoofs with oil till they glistened.

Color sergeants uncased the Stars and Stripes and the scarlet banner which bore the regiment's coat of arms, and the battery guidons fluttered free. Up ahead the drums beat, the bugles blew a march, and the regiment rolled forward.

Johnny Brent, riding beside his platoon, cocked his campaign hat at an old-timer's angle. Settling his automatic against his hip, he pulled down the skirts of his overcoat and glanced proudly at the red numerals of the regiment on his saddlecloth. Barbara, skittish with spirits, arched her neck and danced to the music of the bugles. At the sound of hoofs behind, Brent had to rein her in tightly or she would have galloped to the head of the column, where she seemed to think she belonged.

Colonel Mack, riding up with his Adjutant, spoke.

"You can manage that mare, can't you, Mr. Brent?"

"Yes, sir."

"There will be no runaways in this parade," the C.O. announced sternly. "In the Victory Parade here in Washington after the Civil War the mount of General Custer bolted. They say it was a magnificent sight. Custer, with his yellow hair streaming and his horse at a dead gallop, stole the show. There's some doubt whether it was an accident. However, Custer got away with it. He was a general. But a second lieutenant—" The military mustache bristled and the Colonel rode on.

Now the regiment was swinging into Pennsylvania Avenue, and the band blared forth with all the capacity of its lungs. The famous thoroughfare echoed to stirring strains written long ago in the Philippines by a young artillery lieutenant who loved his arm of the service— *The Caisson Song.*

> *Over hill, over dale,*
> *We have hit the dusty trail,*
>   *And those caissons go rolling along. . . .*

The wheels of the gray guns rumbled an accompaniment, and hoofs beat an obbligato. Hearts leaped high, not only those of every soldier, sitting straight and silent, but of the cheering crowds lining the route. Johnny Brent, stealing a look toward a stand, caught his mother's eyes shining out on him from the throng. He gulped and turned away to watch the intervals of his platoon. Barbara, stepping high and proudly, caracoled under him. "Look!" she seemed to convey. "Don't we make a gallant sight, marching off to war!"

It was only one regiment of field artillery, but it *was* a gallant sight. The long column stretching down the Avenue—the grim, businesslike guns of the firing batteries, the ammunition sections, the mule-drawn, canvas-covered supply wagons, reminiscent of the prairie schooners of the pioneers—the few older officers and sergeants who had seen action in past wars and the set, earnest faces of the young men who were still to stand fire—the teams of willing horses, shoulders in their collars, doing their share. In full blast, the band played on.

> *Then it's hi! hi! hee!*
> *The Field Artillery.*
>   *Sound off your numbers loud and strong.*
> *Where e'er you go,*
> *You will always know*
>   *That those caissons are rolling along.*

Johnny Brent's knees gripped his mount. He could sense that she felt it, too,—the heart-lifting summons of this martial music, prelude to battle. This parade was the beginning of a long march which would bring the regiment in the face of the enemy in far-away France. Then, under the conditions of modern warfare, the band would be silent, its members serving as stretcher-bearers. But as it played now, so must the Seventh Cavalry's brass have blared *Garry Owen* on a bitter cold day back in the '70's, when Custer charged a Cheyenne village on the Washita —playing the Seventh into action until instruments froze.

The music ceased. The regiment turned homeward.

Back in camp again, Lieutenant Brent rode toward his battery area. Leaning down over the neck of his mount, he patted her and spoke softly into one ear, "Barbara, you sure were stepping in that parade. You looked like pretty near the whole show to me."

The mare flipped an ear further back toward his voice. What female does not love flattery?

"Yes," her rider went on, "you were the belle of the ball."

But now Barbara's ears pricked forward. They were passing the mess hall. Outside the kitchen a lonely figure sat peeling potatoes. Barbara craned her neck toward him and whinnied. Jim Thomas grinned at her; then his gaze shifted to the man on her back and there was hatred in that level, scowling stare.

"*Whew!*" Johnny Brent said under his breath. How viciously that fellow had stabbed a spud in the pan in his lap! Looked as if he wished it had been a certain officer. Certainly in the days of old, men had killed each other in quarrels over a horse. Maybe they still did in the West.

"Forget it, Brent," Johnny warned himself. "There goes your romantic imagination again. This is 1918. All you did was exercise an officer's privilege. If somebody ranks you out of the mare, it's to be hoped you take it better than that sourpuss on K.P."

But his conscience hurt him. The incident had taken all the triumph out of the day.

While he was standing back of the picket line, supervising the grooming, he saw Barbara's ears go up again. A second later he identified the distant sound she had caught as the sputter of a motorcycle speeding into camp. After an interval a bugle sounded Officers' Call.

"Hey!" Sergeant Quinn exclaimed with sudden interest. "A courier and then Officers' Call at this time iv day. Somethin's up! The lootenant had better be dusting over to Headquarters."

Assembled at Headquarters, the officers of the regiment faced Colonel Mack eagerly. The old terror allowed a period of tantalizing silence to elapse. Then with the slow, precise diction he used so that no one could claim to have misunderstood him, he spoke:

"Gentlemen, I have received the following secret and confidential orders. . . ."

Orders overseas! At last! The Colonel spoke on unhurriedly. Entrainment in two days for a port of embarkation—meaning Hoboken. Guns and other wheeled equip-

Barbara craned her neck and whinnied

ment to be turned in. The regiment would be given the splendid French 75 mm. guns on the other side. Abruptly the speaker broke off.

"And the horses, sir?" a major asked.

"I regret to say," Colonel Mack resumed gravely, "that they, too, are to be turned in. Tomorrow a remount detail will pick them up for shipment overseas from Baltimore. Whether we'll get them back on the other side, I don't know. I'll do what I can. They're fine animals, and we've trained them well. Too bad but— That will be all, gentlemen."

Johnny Brent strode excitedly back to his tent. Off to war at last. What grand news that was! Of course it was a darned shame about the horses. Tough to lose Barbara.

There was a scratch on his tent flap. On his invitation the new stable orderly entered and reported that Stable Sergeant Quinn requested the lieutenant's presence on the line to look over a horse with colic. Brent grinned. Quinn was only after the news, but the officer walked down to the line.

Quinn's Irish map was bright with expectation. "We're off, ain't we, sor?" he asked. "Hope it ain't no wild rumor this time."

"Sergeant Quinn, I have nothing to say except that the grapevine in this outfit works like lightning. By the way, if we ever did get orders overseas, I understand we'd have to turn in our horses."

"Ain't that the Army for yuh?" Quinn exclaimed. "After all the training we done on 'em! Any chance iv our gitting 'em back over there?"

"One in a thousand. Can't tell whether they'll go to an American, French or British outfit. We might never get any horses. I heard tell we might even be motorized."

Quinn's eyes turned heavenward. "The saints preserve us from the likes of that!" he petitioned.

"Amen!" said Brent. Glancing toward the picket line, his eyes lit on Barbara. "I hate to lose her," he said sadly.

A soldier stepped out from behind Quinn's tent.

"Know what it's like now, don't you?" snapped Jim Thomas.

"Spying, was you?" growled Sergeant Quinn.

"Hadn't noticed you stopping at anything, Sarge," came the retort. "You can go hang, the two of you and your blasted Army! Go hang with your outfit of flivver artillery! I'm pulling up stakes!"

"You try going over the hill and see what happens to yuh!" Quinn threatened.

"Hold on," Brent interposed. "I'm sorry things worked out the way they have."

"Yeah." The twisted look on Thomas's face was bitter.

"Wait. We're bound for a big fight. Know what a man who deserted just before we sailed would be called, don't you? Yellow!"

Jim Thomas's hard fists doubled. "No man's going to call me yellow." His voice was low but deadly.

Brent looked him straight in the eyes. "And I'm not calling you yellow—yet," he said.

For a moment the Texan stood stock-still. Then he turned and strode rapidly away. Barbara neighed after him.

Fighting blood

5: DEATH IN THE DARK

> *Far off a solitary trumpet blew.*
> *Then waiting by the doors the war-horse neigh'd*
> *As at a friend's voice.*
>
> <div align="right">TENNYSON: <i>Guinevere</i></div>

ONCE more the chestnut mare found herself penned with thousands of her kind. The corrals at the port of Baltimore, where the regiment's horses had been sent, were as packed as those at the Kansas City Remount Depot had been. Many a time in the past four years had they been filled thus, emptied and filled again, with cavalry mounts for Palestine and Mesopotamia, artillery teams for the Western Front, and mules to pull machine gun carts and supply wagons. "More, send us more," had been the urgent cry of the Allies, as the war's toll of animals, like that of the men they served, had risen into the millions. The American Army, shipping now for its own needs, would add 68,000 more horses and mules to the long procession which clattered up gangplanks or were hoisted into holds for a voyage and an adventure from which few ever would return.

And again the constant movement of many horses presented an illusion, but here, in the twilight, not of a grain field but of an expanse of the restless sea they must cross. Barbara was nervous, as she had been months before. Alert and wary of a bite or kick from some evil-tempered horse, she threaded her way here and there, as if she were seeking someone. She missed the uncrowded picket line back at camp, and it was about this time that Jim Thomas used to come from mess with sugar or a slice of apple for her. Stroking her ears or scratching her jaw most delightfully, he would stand there for a long while and talk to her. Who shall say she did not understand? Surely no horseman who has known the keen intelligence of a noble animal—the swift response to voice and hand and knee—the instant, uncanny perception of his moods of confidence or fear, displeasure or affection. It is close to speech, this wordless communication, and surely the basis for Homer's tale that when Achilles reproached his chariot team for carrying his friend Patroclus to his doom, the horse Xanthus, empowered by the goddess Hera, spoke and warned his master of his own approaching death.

A subtle menace spread through the air now. Barbara seemed to sense it, for she raised her head the better to see over the taller animals around her. Would that man she loved never come? Never before had he failed her. Never before had she needed him so. At last she lifted her muzzle and whinnied plaintively. Through the corrals other lonely horses answered, yet no familiar figure in a uniform appeared. Several corrals away a sleepy sentry swore at the neighing.

Dusk deepened into the black of a moonless night. In the shadows of buildings near the corrals, four stealthy shapes merged into a whispering group. They were almost invisible, for they wore dark clothes and their faces were ebony. A glimmer of lights on whites of eyes and teeth might have revealed four Negroes, but lights were few and far away. One Negro loosened the stopper of a bottle in his pocket. The other three produced small glass phials. Handling them gingerly, they stuck the needles of hypodermic syringes through the corks and slowly filled them, pulling out the plungers.

"Git goin'," ordered the big black man who was the leader. "Couldn't have no better night."

True, the night was ideal for their purpose. The heavy-set captain of the German merchant marine, who had hired the Negroes, always sent them out on these expeditions on such nights. Hidden in a Baltimore flat, the captain, a chief of the German sabotage and spy systems in the United States, awaited the return and report of his agents. This should prove a fine night's work in the service of the *Vaterland*.

Some forty miles away a second German, a young scientist, also was admiring the quality of the night as he entered a house on the outskirts of Washington. Locking doors and seeing that blinds were well drawn, he switched on the lights in a well-equipped laboratory. With the skill and care learned in an American university, he busied himself with tubes and retorts in which he was growing deadly, teeming germ cultures. Demand for them by the captain and his gangs of white and black men raiding the ports and remount depots was heavy. Loads for their sharp hypos must not be lacking.

Because of these secret servants of the Kaiser, many an Allied battery and machine gun company had waited in vain for horse and mule replacements. Not until long after the war would the American authorities learn of the extent of their operations or of the existence of the germ-culture laboratory so near the nation's capital.

Now the Negroes had reached the corrals undetected. The man with the bottle emptied it into a watering trough. Every horse that drank of its poisoned contents would contract the highly destructive and contagious disease of glanders. Jaw glands hardened, mucous membranes painfully ulcerated, many of the poor beasts would droop with dumb suffering and die. The black men with the syringes crept toward horses standing near the corral fences.

At the approach of the big leader, horses, vaguely alarmed, moved back a little. Swearing under his breath, the Negro climbed astride the fence. He was taking no chances on entering the corral and being kicked when he jabbed. From a pocket of his coat, he took a handful of oats and extended it, speaking softly. The horses stood, sniffing suspiciously. Finally a small mare stepped hesitantly forward.

Barbara was hungry. Larger horses had crowded her out at feeding time, and she had garnered only a few wisps of hay. Those oats smelled good. "Come an' git it, li'l hoss," the Negro crooned.

With a handful of grain like this, Jim Thomas had sometimes called her to him. No bitter experience with man's treachery lurked in Barbara's memory. Yet some instinct made her mistrustful. She halted. Then the fragrance of oats stole into her nostrils and she could no longer resist. She walked up and dipped into the offering.

With infinite caution the man's free left hand secured a grip on her headstall. Barbara stood still, munching.

A right hand drew forth the hypodermic needle. Fingers found the plunger bars. An air bubble appeared at the needle point. Back of it, ready for ejection, lurked a charge of anthrax bacilli. Once in the veins, that microscopic death would burn them out with fatal fever fires.

The hand poised, swooped down at the mare's neck. Only just in time Barbara's eyes caught the motion. She jerked back and the needle missed.

But the would-be killer was a tremendously powerful man. He had a firm hold on the headstall and a crook of his arm around a fence post gave him purchase. Barbara, straining, could not wrench loose.

"Ah'll fix yo', yo' runty, li'l—" The needle arm swept up again to stab.

The whites of the mare's eyes rolled upward. Frantically she twisted her head.

Across the centuries, the blood of mighty war horses, her forebears, surged up within her—blood of the battle mares of Ramases and Mohammed, of the steeds of Cortez, trained to bite the foe in the thick of the fray. The little chestnut sank her teeth deep into a black forearm.

A yelp of agony shattered the stillness of the night. The big Negro flung himself backward off the fence and, joined by the others, rushed off in the darkness. Shouts for the corporal of the guard rose from the corral sentries.

Barbara, trembling with anger and fear, thrust back into the snorting herd.

She hung between heaven and hell.

6: BELOW DECKS

Wave the green flag! Let them go!—
Only horses? Yes, I know;
But my heart goes down the line
With them, and their grief is mine!—
There goes honour, there goes faith,
Down the way of dole and death,
Hidden in the cloud that clings
To the battle-wrath of kings!

W. H. OGILVIE: *The Remount Train*

WAR HORSE

So come with us, buckskin and sorrel,
  And come with us, skewbald and bay:
Your country's girth-deep in the quarrel,
  Your honour is roped to the fray:
Where flanks of your comrades are foaming
  'Neath saddle and trace-chains and band,
We look for the Kings of Wyoming
  To speak for the sage-brush and sand.
W. H. OGILVIE: *A Call to the Cow Ponies*

THE tang of the sea and all the distinct smells of the water front filled the nostrils of the horses led down to the docks. Here were smells, and sights and sounds, too, utterly unfamiliar to them. And yet they may have felt such vague, faint stirrings of memory as a man does sometimes in strange surroundings—a tingling in the veins which seems to say: "Here have I, or some of the same blood as I, passed before."

So they went down to the sea in ships, retracing a voyage their ancestors had made. The big steamship waiting to embark them testified to their vital importance. Provision must be made for them, no less than for troops and munitions, out of shipping desperately limited through sinkings by German submarines. A horse requires ten tons of cargo space, and this vessel, which carried 500 animals, might have transported ten times as many men. Its assignment to the willing animals that kept the caissons rolling along was a real tribute.

There seemed to be no end to the strange and unnerving experiences Barbara must undergo. First, that night of terror in the corral. Then, yesterday, she and all the other horses selected for shipment had been given the invaluable Mallein test for glanders; animals with a positive reaction had been hastily isolated to prevent the spreading of the disease. A group of veterinaries closely examined the chestnut mare and the rest, taking temperatures, noting pulses, counting respirations and palpating various glands. No more thorough a going-over was given soldiers entering the service.

Now, on the day of embarkation, Barbara was led toward a tower-steel crane. Nervously she submitted while men fastened under her belly something that felt like an extra large surcingle. It was a sling of webbing. The men stepped back and signaled. With a raucous whirring and grinding, the engine of the crane started, and the terrified little mare was swept up toward the sky. For an awful moment she hung between heaven and hell. Then she descended into the black depths of the hold where, unslung, she was led panting into a stall and tied.

She may well have believed she was in hell during the twenty days of that stormy voyage. The rolling and pitching of the ship made it difficult for her to keep her feet, and often she was afraid to lie down. With hatches battened down, the air, bad enough anyway with disinfectant and the ammoniacal odor of dung, grew almost unbearably foul, and there was no blower system. A seasick horse detail, struggling to water and feed with bran and hay, could cope but little with cleaning up the stalls. That lower deck became an Augean stables, and there was no Hercules aboard.

But Barbara was lucky in the warmth of the hold. It was on the drafty upper deck that pneumonia broke out. While strenuous efforts by a capable veterinary controlled it to some extent, more than twenty carcasses went over the side.

Perhaps it was some of the carcasses, which broke loose from weights and floated to the surface, that betrayed the convoy. Perhaps it was a gleam of light aboard a ship; even the glow of a cigarette might catch the eye of an alert submarine commander, peering through his periscope. Whatever the betrayal that night in the Irish Channel, a torpedo crashed into the vessel ahead of the horse transport. The U-boat captain, finger on trigger, lined his sights on the steamer following for the load in his second tube.

Down on the lower deck, the horses were gripped with the terror that swept through the ship. Barbara, flung from one side of her stall to the other by the zigzag course, snorted in panic. Half muffled, ominous, the booms of rapid gunfire penetrated to the hold. If any men had been confined in that gloom, bound and helpless, the horror of their impending fate might have driven them mad. Mercifully, the horses could only vaguely sense threatening danger. Spared the curse of human imagination, they could not envision water flooding in and submerging them while, struggling and wild-eyed, they tugged at ropes and iron rings as their prison sank with them to the bottom of the sea. How narrowly that doom was escaped was measured by a foaming, white wake a few yards astern where the torpedo rushed by.

When the ship ceased shaking under the reverberation of depth charges dropped by escorting destroyers, Barbara gradually quieted. As in the corral at Baltimore with the hypo of anthrax poised over her, she had been close to death—and she would face it again. But her experience in the sling when she was hoisted aboard still remained her most fearsome memory.

She was forced to endure that ordeal again when the convoy docked safely at Brest. Disembarked, overjoyed at being on firm ground once more, the column of horses was led toward a remount depot. They shied when trucks rumbled past them, but when drays, drawn by huge French Percherons, passed, some of the heavy wheel horses in the column neighed a friendly greeting, for here were kin of theirs. Their line had been bred from Percheron stallions, imported to the United States and crossed with native stock, and to them they owed their mighty sinews.

On the very day that the horses were landed at Brest, the troop transport carrying Barbara's regiment docked at Le Havre. Marched through a dismal drizzle of rain, the regiment was quartered in a so-called rest camp on a wind-swept hill. In the orderly room in the front of the Head-quarters hut, a smart-looking soldier was on duty. The cord of artillery red around his campaign hat was neat and unfaded. His uniform had been refitted to him by the bat-tery tailor. The lamplight glistened on the polish of his pistol holster and the leather inset in his canvas leggings.

Jim Thomas relaxed, having just saluted a staff officer from G.H.Q. and ushered him to see Colonel Mack. Well, he reflected, here he was in France. Of course he had not been able to take a taunt of being yellow from that shave-tail, Brent. Queer, it had been that selfsame bird who had complimented him on his appearance at inspection today and detailed him to act as regimental orderly. Trying to square himself, Thomas supposed, though he ought to have sense enough to know it couldn't be done.

Idly the orderly began listening to the murmur of talk from the inner room.

"So we're to entrain for Valdahon," he heard the Colo-nel's distinct accents. "Where is that?"

"South of France. French artillery school," the staff man answered. "Your regiment will train there on the 75's."

The Colonel's next words made Jim sit up suddenly.

"We had a fine lot of horses in the States," said the Colonel. "It's entirely possible they may have been shipped over just about this time. By their hoof numbers and record cards we probably could identify most of them. I would like to prefer a request that those horses of ours be reassigned to us."

Thomas, listening harder than ever, grinned happily. But the grin faded to a look of sadness at the staff officer's next words.

"Sorry, sir. You'll be issued no horses until your regiment's training at Valdahon has been completed. In spite of all we've shipped, horses are badly needed right now. Spain is being scoured for 'em. Our Allies want every nag they can lay hands on. When we get more troops over here, the French promise to turn over all the animals they can, and the British say they'll spare us a pair from every artillery team of theirs, if necessary."

"I see," the Colonel said.

"As for that lot of yours, if they're here, they'll go into the pool, and who knows what will become of 'em?" the staff officer finished.

With a helpless gesture, Private Thomas resumed his post.

Strangers, always strangers. Barbara, ill at ease, was continually looking for the men she had grown to know —Thomas, Lieutenant Brent, Sergeant Quinn. They had been good to her, and the mass herding and casual care she had received since did nothing to ease her homesickness for them. The affections of a horse are less easily engaged than those of a dog and are always less apparent, for the Creator has endowed the dog with all but speech, particularly in the eloquence of its tail. Yet a horse, given love and understanding, makes known that its own are pledged in return, even unto death. Thus it was that General Lee's iron-gray charger, *Traveller*, led in procession to his master's grave, lowered his muzzle to the flower-covered bier and whinnied a last farewell.

Barbara had been made much of, had been treated as a pet in the months she had served with the regiment. She could not forget. Small wonder that now she stood with drooping head, like an animal with distemper. No one noticed her.

If Santa Barbara, patron of the artillery, may be deemed to have watched over the chestnut mare, her namesake, now she withdrew her protection, for the mare, cut out of the herd with a number of other single mounts to fill out a consignment on a French purchase, was transferred to the cavalry.

It was a proud, old regiment she joined. Its squadrons had thundered in review before the great Napoleon, and its banners were blazoned with his victories. In every war since, it had acquitted itself honorably, even in the disastrous defeat of 1870. In this war it had helped turn back the Germans at the Marne. Although subsequent stabilization of the front by trench warfare had relegated all cavalry to the rear areas much of the time, this regiment never had ceased to serve strenuously. Courier duty, guarding prisoners and trench digging had fallen to its lot. Thrice, with high hopes, it had ridden forward, ready to charge through an expected gap in the enemy's front —break-throughs that never came. It was on the second of those occasions that the regiment, concentrated in a wood, had been caught by shellfire and suffered the severe casualties which had necessitated the present replacements in men and horses.

Again Barbara found herself on a picket line where a choice of mounts was being made. Neither she nor the other horses showed up well after the voyage and the boxcar trip to the French cavalry depot.

"They send us their dregs now, the Americans," ran repeated mutters of men inspecting the line.

At last an arm in horizon blue reached forward to untie Barbara.

"Here, Vallon," called a troop commander. "Best choose this mare."

A heavy-set man advanced. Although he was middle-aged, he wore the chevrons of an *aspirant*, a grade between non-commissioned rank and lieutenant; there were not a few older men in junior ranks in the French Army. He was continually wetting his lips under his heavy mustache and in back of his eyes was a hunted look.

"Name of a name!" he swore. "Must I ride that insect,

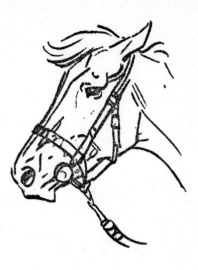

Barbara, eyes rolling sprang back.

mon Capitaine?"

"She'll carry you," his superior promised. "There's good blood in her. Besides, there is little choice left."

"Little choice," Vallon echoed in a surely tone. "For want of a better, then," he grumbled and beckoned a trooper to lead the mare away.

On his own troop's line, the *Aspirant* again examined his mount with growing disfavor.

"Such is the beast left to me after the officers of St. Cyr skim the cream," he growled. "Behold my charger! Species of a camel!"

His anger was mounting. He glanced around and saw no one. Glaring at Barbara, he spat at her slender fore-legs and cried hoarsely:

"You'll carry me, will you? You'd best or I'll beat the life out of you!"

With that he swung back his arm and slapped the mare heavily on the side of the head.

Barbara, eyes rolling, sprang back, tugging against her tie-rope.

Concealed in a doorway, two troopers, a veteran and a recruit, were watching. The recruit started forward.

"The dirty pig!" he exclaimed. "To treat thus an un-offending animal!"

"Be tranquil," warned the veteran, pulling him back. "Learn never to interfere with an officer, my little one. Also, you do not know about Vallon. When a Boche shell bursts beside you, as by him, you may understand."

"Shell-shocked!" the recruit whispered.

"But yes, and badly. He cannot always keep control of himself. Yet he continues to serve."

"I understand," said the recruit. "But I pity the horse."

"*C'est la guerre*," the other answered with a shrug.

Pity could not help Barbara. She was at the mercy of a man whose strained and tortured nerves vented themselves in outbursts of cruelty, except when he was restrained by observing eyes. By right Vallon should have been in a hospital, but the shell which had exploded so near him had given him no visible wound. He would have no one calling him a coward or an *embusqué*, so he stayed on duty. Every day he grew more tense, irritable, suspicious of slights. The overwrought state of the rider communicated itself to the finely-strung mount. Barbara never felt the too-heavy body of the *Aspirant* settle in the saddle that she did not wince and begin to quiver in anticipation of the mistreatment she had come to expect.

The willing little mare tried hard, nevertheless. Quickly she picked up cavalry drill, though she missed the familiar rumbling of the guns and caissons. She learned not to shy at the rasp and flash of drawn sabres. When the band played the martial measures of the *Sambre et Meuse*, or the mounted bugle corps tossed their instruments high in the air, caught them and sounded a flourish, Barbara almost recaptured her gayety and began to curvet. Then the bit would jerk savagely in her tender mouth and sharp spurs dig into her flanks, as Vallon cursed her and the racket.

Now it is true that horses of the Arab blood, with its trait of intelligence, are docile and faithful when kindly and understandingly treated. Under cruelty, their finely-strung nervous systems rebel and they become untractable and vicious. Or, their spirits broken, they sicken and die. By the barbarities of her shell-shocked master, Barbara was doomed to one or the other of those fates, and it drew closer with the passage of every day.

Old friends had not forgotten the chestnut mare, but they were faraway in the south of France.

Stable Sergeant Quinn stood beside a 75 mm. gun and patted the breech of that graceful, deadly cannon—buff, brown, green, and yellow in the motley of its camouflage.

"A swate little piece of pipe, sor," he remarked to Lieutenant Brent. "But what's the likes o' this to a stable sergeant? If it gits anything wrong with it, even that dumb Scandahoovian of a chief mechanic iv ourn can tinker it inter shape. It can't have nothing like fistulous withers nor a foine, flatulant colic what takes some real fixing. Nor can it be after moving out by itself."

Brent laughed. "We ought to be getting some horses soon," he said. "I sort of miss 'em."

Captain Carrick, the battery commander, called from

across the gun park and beckoned. The two hurried toward him.

"Horses!" he announced excitedly. "Horses for the whole outfit coming in. Got to make a good choice for the battery, Sergeant. Come along. You, too, Brent." He strode rapidly ahead.

Quinn's blue eyes were alight. "Does the lootenant think there might be—somewhere in this lot—an—"

"An old pal of ours," Brent smiled back. "Maybe. There's a bare chance. We'll go through 'em with a fine tooth-comb. If the mare's there, just let some other battery try to snag her away from us. I hope she is there. If she is, we'll get the Padre to burn a candle to Santa Barbara in thanksgiving."

"*Ora pro nobis*," murmured Sergeant Quinn earnestly.

"Second the motion," Johnny Brent responded. Then he halted abruptly with the thought that struck him. "Sergeant," he ordered, "get Private Thomas over here right away!"

"What? Him?" Quinn was dumbfounded.

"Yes. He knows Barbara better than either of us. Don't you see, if one of us doesn't spot her quick in this bunch, some other battery will grab her."

Quinn saw two D Battery privates and sent them off at the double. Soon the Texan was there, saluting.

"Sir, Private Thomas reports as ordered." His face was mask-like and his eyes hard, as always when he met Brent.

Quickly, eagerly, Brent explained the situation. "Help us see if Barbara's here," he urged. "I'm not ordering," he finished, "I'm asking you."

"And I'm beggin' yuh, m' boy," Sergeant Quinn added.

"Want her for some more horse trading, Sergeant?" Jim sarcastically demanded. But he hastened to the lines.

There the best horsemen of all the batteries were making strenuous tours of inspection to spot the best animals before the choosing began. The new horses were a mixed lot. Among them were rejects by the Allies. Clearly they were not up to the horses the regiment had turned in at home. But many were American, as "U.S." on the hoofs testified, and they would do.

Jim Thomas's anxious scrutiny of the hundreds on the lines was painstakingly thorough. Finally the three from Battery D met.

"Couldn't find her," Brent declared.

"Not hide nor hair iv her," Sergeant Quinn corroborated.

"She's not here." Jim Thomas was positive.

The three men looked at each other. An electric spark of sympathy passed between them. Jim barely caught himself joining in the others' sighs.

He stifled it off, came to attention.

"Anything further, Lieutenant?" he asked stiffly.

"No, but thank you," Brent replied. Formally and coldly, he returned the salute.

Strangers

7: HORSE, FOOT, AND DRAGOONS

> With click of hoof and toggle chain,
> The battery rolls on again,
>   Rolls on to war.
> The guidon sheathes its tell-tale red,
> On toward the rumbling up ahead,
> The battery rolls on, rolls on to war.

Gun and caisson galloping on,
Teams with their traces tight.
Through the maze of a dust-cloud's haze,
Unlimber! and Action right!
Range dial spun, flash of a gun,
Scream of a shell set free
From the wheeled guns, the steeled guns
Of the Field Artillery!

FAIRFAX DOWNEY: *The Battery Rolls On*

THE roads through the ancient forest were like dank, dark corridors in a dungeon. Rain filtered through the leaves of oaks and beeches, their overhanging branches deepening the gloom of a moonless night. The blackness seemed almost palpable to the marching men groping through it.

Up to the Front again. It was an old story now to Lieutenant John Brent, riding at the head of his battery's combat train. It seemed so long ago that the regiment had left Valdahon and first gone into the line, although that was in March and this was only mid-July. Stirring action has been packed into those weeks. First the quiet sector east of Verdun, which had livened up considerably; then the terrific fighting at Belleau Wood, when the German drive had been halted and rolled back; and now, after a brief rest, a forced march of two nights and a day, to take part in an attack which gave every evidence of being another big show.

Brent's weary mount stumbled and almost went down. He muttered imprecations and from the first section behind heard himself echoed by Caisson Corporal Thomas, whose horse also had nearly fallen. The same thought was in both men's minds. Each was wishing a certain sure-footed little mare were under him. From the rear boomed the strident tones of First Sergeant McNally, ordering spare cannoneers off the limbers to strain at the wheels of a carriage which had slipped from the crown of the road into the clinging mud of the ditch.

Slowly the column moved forward.

"Walk 'em out," Brent called back.

The regiment's guns were in position, but its combat trains must bring them more ammunition for the dawn barrage and the heavy firing of the expected advance.

To the left of the artillery column, the shadowy figures of infantry struggled on, each file with a hand on the shoulder of the man ahead to maintain contact in the en-shrouding blackness.

What turmoil the primeval Forêt de Retz hid in its depths that night! Thousands upon thousands of troops, their guns, tanks, trucks, and ambulances jamming and clogging and pressing on again through its tunnel-like roads. There streamed the units of two veteran divisions of American Regulars. Between them, to form with them the spearhead of the attack, marched the famous First Moroccan Division of the French, with its dreaded Moors and black Senegalese and the fierce Foreign Legion. Part of a far-flung battle line, they strove onward, alternately cursing and blessing the darkness that at once hampered them and concealed them from the unsuspecting foe. Swiftly the night dwindled toward dawn. At the edge of the forest, Brent, with a thrill of admiration, watched a company of Marines of his division debouch from another road. The exhausted men were pushing forward at a run in order to reach their jump-off point for the attack on time.

The artillery was ready, in position. Behind a crest stretched a long line of 75's, almost hub-to-hub, and in rear of them, prepared to fire over them, were ranked the 155 mm. howitzers. For miles along the eastern face of the forest and to its flanks was ranged this tremendous concentration of cannon. Back of the field pieces, crews manned the heavier guns and railroad artillery, and forward were emplaced trench mortars, one-pounders, heavy and light machine guns. Laid and loaded, unseen, black muzzles with death in their throats gaped toward the German lines, awaiting the hour.

Beside D Battery, Brent saw Captain Carrick waving him on.

"Unload those shells and fuses in a hurry," the Battery Commander ordered. "We open fire in fifteen minutes. Get back to the reserve dump as fast as you can and bring up more ammunition. We'll be moving forward and we'll need it."

Brent took his empty caissons back at a gallop. In the

woods he glanced at his wrist watch. It was 4: 34. One minute more. Time seemed suspended in a breathless hush. Somewhere in the depth of the forest a bird started to sing —a long, trilling note that never was finished.

Ten thousand thunderclaps reverberated at once. The earth and the air shook under the shattering, deafening conclusion of those massed guns roaring into action. The infantry sprang to their feet and plunged forward. Before them rolled the barrage, rending and smashing the German trenches. The battle of Soissons had begun.

Never afterwards could Johnny Brent bring back more than fragmentary, jumbled memories out of the smoke and confusion of that great battle which was the turning point of the war. It was as if he had seen all of it, as he did part, through the blurred eye-pieces of his gas mask— "through a glass darkly." Its panorama unrolled like a swiftly-run motion picture reel, for this was open warfare, with the guns no longer standing fast in emplacements and firing by the map. Batteries galloped forward, unlimbered and with open sights poured volleys into the retreating enemy.

Forward, always forward. Constant calls for more ammunition. Brent and the combat train, following the guns, passed long, field-gray columns of prisoners, herded to the rear. Yet vengefully, stubbornly, the Germans fought back with machine guns and artillery. Up ahead Brent watched C Battery climb over a crest. No sooner had its young commander at its head showed against the skyline than the blinding flash of a bursting shell enveloped him. "A battery seen is a battery lost," runs an old artillery maxim. But the first section chief, taking command, wheeled the column back under cover.

Now the path of the advance was strewn with dead and wounded. The combat train, threading its way between them, must drive with infinite care and skill. Magnificently the horses, frightened though they were by the shells bursting around them, responded to rein and pressure of leg. Once a riderless steed, galloping toward the train for company in its terror, was struck by a shell fragment fifty metres away and dropped, kicking in agony. Brent never forgot how Thomas swung down from his saddle as the train passed at a gallop and put a bullet from his automatic between the suffering animal's eyes.

The crashing din of the battle roared onward under the July sun. Now the red haze of blood and sweat and smoke and weariness lifted only for the thrill of combat, for moments when death passed close or for some such relief of stress as Sergeant Quinn's appearance on a dirty white horse when he moved the *echelon* forward.

"What do you mean coming up on a white horse, Sergeant?" an officer bawled him out. "You'll draw the fire of every German gun in the sector!"

"Sure, sor," Quinn apologized. "When I rode this baste inter thim woods last night he was a roan. All that rain bleached him. How was I to be knowing the hide iv him was dyed?"

"Well, get him out of here, *quick*," the officer ordered. Quinn ranked a corporal out of his mount, and the corporal walked until he caught a loose horse.

The German Army, that splendid fighting machine, resisted valorously but, surprised and overwhelmed, it gave way before the spirited assault of the American and French divisions. Back ebbed the disorganized German battle line until the attacking battalions, fast though they moved, could no longer maintain touch. In the Allied posts of command, where breathless runners brought reports, they spoke elatedly of a real break-through.

It was then that Lieutenant Brent, on his way forward late in the afternoon with yet more ammunition, glanced back over his shoulder at the edge of the Forêt de Retz and beheld an unforgettable spectacle. Emerging from the screen of the trees were long lines of horsemen—a brigade of French cavalry. They came on at a trot, regiments of lancers and dragoons in column of squadrons, wave on wave of horizon blue. Fresh and trim, riding as if on parade, they swept ahead, ranks opening to pass the American combat train's weary drivers and foam-flecked teams. So, thought Johnny Brent, must the Light Brigade have looked, advancing to launch its historic charge at Balaklava.

Engulfed by horsemen, the American officer looked for

a moment into the eyes of a pleasant-faced French lieutenant, about his own age.

"Good luck," Brent wished him. "*Bon chance.*"

The Frenchman gave him a happy smile. "*Merci bien,
mon vieux,*" he called back.

"*Vive la cavalerie! Vive la France!*" Brent yelled after
him, and the French officer turned in his saddle to salute
and shout back, "*Vive l'Amerique!*"

The rearmost troop was passing now and Brent found
himself gaping at another French officer, an older man,
among the file closers. His body was rigid; his face, set
like a mask, was ghastly white. Unseeing eyes, haunted by
some unspeakable terror, stared straight ahead.

"He's scared to death," said Brent, half aloud. "Shell-
shocked, I bet. But he has nerve. He's sticking it."

A salvo of shrapnel burst overhead, too far to the rear
to do any harm. But Brent saw the receding figure of the
Frenchman shudder convulsively. He spurred his mount
violently, and when the animal leaped forward, reined in
savagely, sawing against its mouth.

Brent gasped. Hoofs clattered behind him and Corporal
Thomas was beside him, his gray eyes burning.

"Did you see her?" he demanded. "See what he done to
her?"

"See *her*? What the devil do you—"

"Barbara! That's Barbara he's riding! I'd know her anywhere."

Why, there *was* something strangely familiar about the little chestnut trotting away out there. Brent, absorbed in the rider, had barely glanced at the horse.

Vehement words were pouring from the usually quiet-spoken Texan. He leaned forward and gathered his reins.

"I'm going to knock that yellow-bellied bully off her!"

"Steady!" the lieutenant spoke sharply. "We don't know that it's Barbara. Anyway, she's a French horse now." He grasped the other's bridle.

"Leggo, you!" Thomas shouted, tugging. "I'll—"

"You'll nothing!" That was big First Sergeant Mc-Nally, who had ridden up on the off side of the corporal. "Get back to your post!"

For a moment Thomas glared wildly at them both. Then, deadly white, he dropped back.

Limp and shaken, Lieutenant Brent halted at the battery position. An uncomfortable incident, that; it might have caused plenty of trouble for a likeable lad. Ordered to replace a wounded officer, he dismounted and sent the combat train to the rear.

The mass of cavalry, nearing the infantry supports, was still in view. The intent artillerymen saw an officer in the van raise an arm. The sun glistened on something slender in his hand. An instant, and that gleam of light was multiplied by a thousand drawn sabres, rising above a falling forest of a thousand lowered, leveled lances.

Flashed all their sabres bare,
Flashed as they turned in air . . .

murmured Johnny Brent, thrilled to the core.

At a gallop the cavalry lunged forward in the charge. They vanished in the field of tall wheat where the front line lay.

"A break-through!" exclaimed the battery commander excitedly. "Send for the limbers. If that cavalry rolls 'em up, we're going straight through to Berlin!"

The last, faint cheer of the charging horsemen seemed still to be lingering in the air when a sinister sound succeeded it. A deadly, distant staccato, as of innumerable pneumatic riveters.

There would be no break-through. Not while German machine guns remained uncaptured.

Johnny Brent was thankful he could not witness that slaughter. Too well could he visualize streams of lead thudding into the ranks of those gallant squadrons—men reeling in their saddles—horses rearing, plunging and going down. Here and there perhaps a machine-gun nest ridden down and gunners lanced and sabered. But always, from flank and front, murderous fire from still more guns that spelled disaster. Surely, he mused, little Barbara and the crazed man who rode her had died valiantly with the rest.

Back through the wheat rode the cavalry—"all that was left of them"—riders with shoulders slumped—troop horses with emptied saddles keeping their place in ranks. Brent could spare them barely a glance, for the battery had flamed into rapid action, taking vengeance on the machine guns, and the German artillery was replying with gas shells mixed with high explosive.

The combat train had been moving slowly to the rear, conserving the strength of the teams. Jim Thomas looked back to see the remnants of the cavalry retreating toward the forest. He scanned every horse with fierce eagerness. Off to the right, on the flank of a shattered troop, he saw a little chestnut in a group of riderless horses.

This time the first sergeant was not quick enough to stop him. He sped away at a dead gallop. As he bore down on them, the French horses also began to run. The few dazed surviving cavalrymen in the group, anxious to reach the shelter of the woods, did not rein in.

Now Thomas was alongside his quarry. It was Barbara without a doubt. Kicking loose from his stirrups, he leaned over toward the running mare and seized her mane and the pommel of her saddle.

The edge of the woods was close now. The galloping horses began to open ranks to thread their way through the trees.

The Texan gathered himself. As his horse and Barbara drew apart, he swung over into her saddle. Pulling her up,

He swung over into Barbara's saddle

he turned her and trotted back to the combat train, bending down to pat her neck.

"You lowdown deserter!" the first sergeant rasped at him. "It's the nearest tree for you."

Thomas looked at him apprehensively, but there was a warm gleam in McNally's icy blue eyes.

"Yep, the nearest tree and a rope," the big man repeated. "A Texas hoss thief alus gits strung up, don't he?"

Mourned a mount killed in action.

8: THE CHANGELING

Now go to the stable,
All you who are able,
And give to your horses
Some oats and some corn.

WAR HORSE

BUGLES, silent at the front, blew once more for the battle-worn regiment withdrawn to a rear area. They blew the flourishes of always-unwelcome Reveille and always-welcome Mess Call. They wailed the sad, sweet notes of Taps, blown either to summon the soldier to rest for the night or for eternity. To many a member of the regiment, turning in at a barn or farmhouse billet, the plaintive call was echoed as a requiem for comrades buried on the battlefield of Soissons.

There were gaps on the picket lines, as in the ranks. "It was the greatest grief to think upon the horses, and the valiant soldiers we had lost." So, four centuries ago, after a battle in Mexico, had written the Conquistador, Bernal Diaz, chronicler of the expedition of Cortez; and now his words were in the hearts of other fighting men in France. Animals which had endeared themselves to the men who cared for them had been killed in action or were dead of wounds or exhaustion. Here a sergeant mourned his lost mount and was not consoled by the prospect of a superior replacement. There a wheel driver sadly groomed a big black whose team-mate was gone; the survivor, restive and lonely, looked constantly about for the companion which had pulled in the traces at his side.

One soldier was enjoying a measure of happiness. Corporal Jim Thomas had his Barbara again. Lovingly he rubbed down her chestnut coat. But his joy was considerably tempered, for she did not remember him. After he had recovered her, there had been five more racking days in the line. He had ridden her as gently as he could but perforce unsparingly. How pitifully she had trembled when he mounted, almost cringing whenever he happened to raise a hand, as if expecting a brutal lacing from a riding crop. Accustomed to the jerk of a curb bit against her raw mouth, she was no longer bridle-wise. Yet even toward the last of the battle, when both rider and horse moved mechanically in a semi-coma of utter weariness, the little mare had responded gallantly.

Until now, when they were back in a rest area, there had been no time to attempt to renew old ties. Soothing her, murmuring to her on the picket line, Thomas strove to win her back. Barbara would turn her head and look at him, but he could find no light of recognition in her eyes. Sometimes slowly, tentatively, a little doubtfully, she stretched her graceful neck toward him. Yet always she shrank away again. Brutality and battle shock had gone deep.

Swallowing his emotion, the Texan saw Stable Sergeant Quinn looking at him.

"Sure 'tis a wonderful thing—love," the sergeant

grinned. "They do say it makes the world go 'round."

"You go to blazes," Thomas muttered.

"The back iv me hand and the sowl iv me foot to you," Quinn retorted. "For all I'm caring, you can go stand a summary court and have your pay stopped a couple years for the loss iv Gover'mint property."

Thomas maintained his sullen silence.

"He don't know what he lost," Quinn persisted in good humor. "I'll have to be telling him. One hoss," he ticked off on his fingers, "abandoned to the Frinch cavalry in retrate."

Thomas continued to ignore him. The stable sergeant flowed on.

" 'Sure,' sez he, 'I trun away that there plug I was riding, but I swapped the baste for this here little beauty of a mare, and a foine trade it was.'

" 'True for you,' sez I, 'but nixt you'll be having to account for wan saddle, bridle, and ither equipment.'

" 'Thim,' sez he, 'was ould stuff, expinded in the Gover'mint service according to regulations. Besides, there was a Frinch officer's saddle on the mare—wan iv thim Sawmure jobs—and worth tin McClellans.'

" 'But,' sez I, 'the likes iv a corp'ral can't be riding that.'

" 'What's to become of it, thin, Quinn, ye ould buzzard?' sez he.

" 'M' boy,' sez I, 'I sold that Frog saddle to wan iv our captuns for *beaucoup francs*.'

" '*Bueno*, Sarge,' sez he in spiggoty. 'The drinks is on me!' "

Quinn grinned with disarming Irish joviality and held out a fat wad of francs.

Gray eyes burning, Jim Thomas flashed back at him.

"Think you can buy me, do you?" he snapped. "Well, you can't! Not after that dirty double-cross you worked on me. But I'll take the money!" He snatched it away. "*You'll* not be drinking it up!"

An expression of deep but comical melancholy overspread Quinn's face. He heaved a vast sigh.

The Texan bore down on Barbara's withers with the brush. She shuddered and jumped. "Sorry, girl," he murmured, patting her. Then he turned angrily on the stable sergeant again.

"Maybe you think I'm sucker enough to fall for your blarney again, Quinn!" he rasped. "Once is plenty. Don't I know that when Brent, wherever he is, shows up, he'll grab the mare away from me again? What if it was me got her back?" he demanded bitterly. "Wasn't it him and McNally wouldn't let me go after her when that Frog cavalryman was roweling her like a greaser full of *mescal*?"

Quinn answered gently. "Sure, I know. But what ilse could he do, lad? Besides, mebbe he won't be back."

"Brent won't? Why not?"

"He got a good whiff iv gas toward the ind iv the show. They packed him off to the hospital."

The Texan's look softened. He remembered the lieutenant through those grueling days at Soissons, galloping up the combat train again and again under heavy shellfire, standing up under it like a man. The guy had nerve. Somehow you couldn't hate him.

"Sorry," he muttered. But a glance at Barbara turned his mood cynical again. "I reckon Brent'll be back," he said, "and I know what he'll do. He'll take the mare. Just the same, I'll take care of her in the meantime. She's taken a terrible beating. I'm going to try to bring her back. She's too good a little horse to let slide to ruination."

"She is that," Quinn said warmly.

Jim's eyes narrowed. "This time, Quinn," he snapped, "I'll not be kidding myself. You can get ready to do some more bootlicking and lay up credit for doing an officer a favor." Quinn's fists clenched, but he took it.

Except for relief from the strain of combat, there was little rest, no idle days, for the regiment. Horses must be watered, fed, groomed and exercised; harness cleaned and oiled; carriages put back into condition; replacements of casualties received. All this activity was for the best, not only because it was necessary but because routine has a blessed effect on overwrought nerves. After regular formations and drill, there were afternoons of swimming in the river and baseball games. Mail from home arrived. So did pay day. Many crisp franc notes went to proprietors of the little cafés in the village who were enriched for life. Others appeared in circles formed in the barn billets, where faint clickings and loud adjurations were heard. Now and again disconsolate soldiers rose with turned-out pockets. Up in a loft a voice sang mournfully:

> *Once a month you sign the payroll.*
> *Cap'n with a list gives you your pay.*
> *You go in the barracks and throw it on a blanket.*
> *Feller says 'Craps!' and takes it all away.*

Inspections, signs of a forthcoming move, were made, and rumors of the next destination of the division flourished like weeds. Every possible source of information was pumped. At the D Battery officers' mess one night, a short first lieutenant, with gray hair and a ruddy outdoor face, was a guest. A "V" superimposed upon the caduceus, the Medical Corps insignia, on his collar, marked him as the veterinary attached to the regiment. Recently returned from a meeting at the Tours Remount Depot, he was the target of his hosts' curiosity.

"Loosen up, Doc," Captain Carrick urged. "Where are we rolling next?"

"Nowhere, unless we get some horse replacements," the guest replied.

"Sure, but we'll get 'em soon, won't we?"

"That depends." The Vet paused significantly. "Guess I'll risk spilling some confidential stuff to you fellows.

Might make you take even better care of your stock than you do."

The A.E.F.'s shortage of animals was critical, he revealed; the shortage amounted to more than 70,000 and that was an improvement, for it had been far worse. Ships for transport across the Atlantic were increasingly scarce. Remount purchases made in Spain, in the face of the strong German influence to contend with there, had yielded only a fair supply. Animal influenza, raging since the past winter, had taken a terrific toll.

"Fact is, our animal transport situation is acute," the Vet continued. "I hear that new artillery regiments back in the States are being motorized."

"There're plenty of places those caterpillar tractors can't go," a lieutenant put in. "We need horses."

"Well, are we getting 'em, Doc?" the battery commander persisted.

"Some," was the reply. "About 13,000 from the British. The French took a census of all their animals not in the Army. There are from three to four hundred thousand, they say, but only about 80,000 can be spared from farming. They're turning about 30,000 over to us—I hope."

"What do you mean, you hope?" somebody asked.

"I mean they'll do it if they don't have high casualties or if something doesn't rile 'em.

"Here's a last tip for you," offered the Vet, rising to go. "Our Brigadier says he's heard the French are sore at our outfit. They claim we've lifted some of their nags off the picket line."

"Rot, that's the old Army game," Captain Carrick snorted. "There never yet was an outfit in the Mounted Service that, given half a chance, didn't swipe a good horse off the next regiment's picket line and leave some old crock in its place. It was a regular pastime down on the Border. I don't doubt we've raided the French a bit and by the same token they've left their calling cards on us."

"Just the same," the Doctor insisted, "the Brigadier is up on his ear. He's invited a Frog general over to inspect our lines and see for himself that we've got no nags that speak French. This battery, of course, will be the picture of innocence." He grinned and waved his hand. "Good evening, gentlemen, and thanks for the chow."

One second lieutenant whispered to another. "Our Brigadier!" he sniffed disrespectfully. "Old Fuss and Feathers! He's a Coast Artilleryman. What's he know about horses?"

"Nothing, I hope," said the other. "But, look here. We'd better pass the word on to Sergeant Quinn. We don't want to lose that neat little chestnut mare we got back at Soissons. Come on."

Quinn listened intently to their story.

"I'll fix it," he promised. "Not only for the sake iv the mare but for that lad, Thomas, who got her back for us. No telling what he'd do if the Frogs spotted Barbara and tried to take her back. He's as like to call an inspector and a couple iv ginerals liars and make a pass at thim. They do tell me there's a military prison in Paris, run by a feller so hardboiled you wished you ain't never been born and gone sojering. Think of being in Paris *and in the jug!* The lootenants can lave it to me."

He hurried to the picket line to find Thomas. Unfortunately he arrived at an inopportune moment.

The Texan's days of patient care at last had won their reward. Rebuffed repeatedly by the mistrust for all mankind Barbara had acquired, he still persisted. Only just now had she remembered the old days and her old master, obscured by recent cruelties. Why, this was the man who always had been good to her. This was the man she loved. Her big eyes dwelt on him for long seconds. Then her velvet muzzle was in his hand, seeking the sugar lump of long ago, now found again.

It was this affecting scene on which Stable Sergeant Quinn had intruded. He gave an apologetic grin and blurted out the warning given him by the officers.

Jim Thomas heard him out; then bent on him a look of cold suspicion.

"Maybe so, maybe not," he said. "*Quien sabe?* If the French don't get her, somebody else will. What's the diff? Reckon I'm through."

With a last look at Barbara, he swung away.

That night Quinn and a farrier worked long over Barbara's brand and hoof marks, translating them from French back into American. Those who know the tricks of the trade can accomplish a certain amount of skulduggery with a hot iron and with a little axel grease, which, filled into hoof brands, may disguise them until they are obliterated by new growth.

They did a pretty fair job. But in his heart Quinn knew it wasn't good enough—not if the inspecting Frenchmen also knew the tricks of the trade.

Down the main street of the village, where headquarters of the Field Artillery Brigade were located, rode a French general. His stature was small but his appearance was martial, even bellicose. Sharp eyes that missed nothing ranged ahead. A dragoon's mustache, large and fierce, spread a canopy over a compressed mouth. Confronted by the ribbons of his decorations, a rainbow would have resigned, and rivaled by the gold braid encircling his cap, the most gorgeous sunset would have given up and called it a day. Most impressive of all was the magnificent charger he bestrode. That was sheer swank, since generals usually rode in limousines, but the mount contributed vastly to the effect and pointed the general's errand. Behind him, instead of the parade which would have been suitable, rode only a single orderly. That soldier did not seem to be aware that he was an anticlimax, for his rubicund visage, a living testimonial to the vintages of France, was beaming.

The general halted in front of headquarters in the *mairie* and glared at the lack of a proper reception. This was unreasonable of him, since he had come an hour before he was expected, but generals can be unreasonable. Plainly disgruntled, he dismounted, turned over his steed to his orderly and entered the building. Thence presently issued the voice of the American general, apologizing in execrable French, and other sounds of confusion and consternation.

For some time the orderly stood to horse in a military manner. Then his roving eye noted a café across the square opening for business. He sniffed, he licked his lips. Conversation inside headquarters gave no signs of slackening and at length the orderly surrendered. Tying the horses to a hitching bar, he disappeared inside the café.

Again the village street resounded to hoofs. Battery D was leading to water, a long column, drivers walking between their pairs. The French horses neighed a greeting as the head of the column appeared.

Toward the head of the battery, Corporal Thomas was marching behind Sergeant Quinn. Simultaneously they sighted the French general's horse. They halted in their tracks and looked at each other. A light of gleeful understanding leaped into their eyes at the same moment. Jim's hostility for the stable sergeant seemed to melt away from him. Acting with perfect teamwork, Quinn ran for the general's charger while Thomas snatched at the halter-shank of the worst horse in the battery.

Even if any of the civilians across the square had been watching, they probably could not have explained how the trick was done. The passing column masked it, as a magician uses a handkerchief to cover sleight-of-hand. The result was sufficiently striking to make anyone stare and rub his eyes. When the tail of the column was past the hitching bar, there where the general's splendid steed had stood, drooped a sorry, bony nag, fit for condemnation. The changeling wore the handsome saddle and bridle which had graced its predecessor.

The battery was out of sight when the French general, accompanied by his American host, and the former's orderly emerged, respectively, from headquarters and café. All three gasped and goggled at the poor bonerack tied to the bar beside the orderly's mount.

A sudden advance of the enemy into that rear area would have caused no wilder alarums and excursions than the wrath of the French general and the angry dismay of Old Fuss and Feathers. With a volley of orders, the Brigadier commanded a minute search of every stable and picket line, beginning with Brigade Headquarters.

The search progressed no further than its starting point. There, crowded into a stall with the Brigadier's own mount, was discovered the French general's charger.

What might have come of this contretemps was never known, for further international complications and a rise

Paul Brown

the General gasped and goggled
on the bone rack

of the Brigadier's already dangerously high blood pressure were prevented by the arrival of horse replacements with orders for the division to entrain immediately for the front. There was no time now for investigations and inspections. With well-disciplined expedition, unit after unit was loaded onto the trains provided.

At the foot of a ramp leading into a box car, Corporal Thomas was gently urging Barbara to enter. The little mare, still nervous, hesitated. Jim caught the eye of the stable sergeant watching him and answered his grin. Somehow he hadn't been able to go on hating the genial Irishman. They had gotten together after their sleight-of-hand with the French general's charger and the liking they had felt for each other in the early days back in Virginia had returned, revived by the bond of men who had seen action together and by their mutual fondness for Barbara. Jim, reassured of Mike Quinn's good faith, had dropped the old grudge. Of course there was still Lieutenant Brent to be considered, but the grapevine had it that he was in pretty bad shape from his gassing and would be invalided and sent home. Thomas even found himself feeling sorry for the officer—at a distance. Patiently he resumed his efforts to lead the mare up the ramp.

"Git going there," Sergeant Quinn called over. "There's a war on."

"Give me a second or two, Sarge," Thomas begged. "I'll make her understand."

"Ain't that mare got eyes?" Quinn demanded. "Look there, right on the side iv the car it says: '*Chevaux* 8— *Hommes* 40.' That means eight horses or forty men."

"Seems like the mare can't read French." Thomas grinned. "I reckon she's not a French horse, after all."

"I ain't so sure." The stable sergeant approached and barked at Barbara. "Hey, *vous. Allez* up there. *Toot sweet!*"

Barbara stood stock-still. Thomas patted her neck and said softly, "Let's go, girl. All aboard."

Barbara docilely walked up the ramp into the car.

"That there," Stable Sergeant Quinn announced with decision, "is an American hoss, and Corporal, don't let nobody tell you different."

*Stood miserably
in the sucking mud.*

9: HOOFPRINTS IN THE MUD

*Now (day and night) unsheltered, in the mud
    You droop and die;
While ruthless hands, for human purpose' sake,
Fashion the complex tools which spill your blood
    And ours in rising flood.*

G. M. JEUDWINE: *War Horses*

WAR HORSE

God speed the horse on the fields of France,
  As he fights in Freedom's name,
God save the horse from the sword and lance
When he bravely halts the foe's advance.
As cannon roar and the shrapnel dance
  Let his stout heart know no shame.
        THOMAS H. HERNDON: *On the Fields of France*

AND the rain fell. Heavy, drenching downpours had scarcely ceased since the regiment detrained far from its destination. Marching by night to escape observation by German planes, by day the batteries lay concealed in dripping woods. Leafy boughs, a screen against eyes in the air, supplied little shelter from the torrents. Knee-deep in mud, the artillerymen struggled through the details of making camp. Even the solace of a more-or-less hot meal from the rolling kitchens was soon forgotten by bedraggled soldiers who wrapped themselves in blankets and *ponchos* and, under gun carriage or pup tent, tried to sleep on the clammy, oozing ground. Tied to wheels, the horses stood miserably, pulling one leg after another out of the sucking mud, as if they were on a vertical treadmill. Before many more days in such watery footing, the soft cartilage of their inner hoofs would begin to rot, and the poor beasts seemed to know it.

Still it rained. One more night, inky as that one before Soissons, brought the batteries near the positions they were to occupy. They turned off the road into a field. Down sank the carriages, almost to their hub caps, in clinging mire. Snorting and panting, the teams heaved against their breast straps, legs driving like piston rods. Here and there a driver's whip whacked an off horse not pulling his share. Cannoneers strained at the wheel spokes. The noncoms rode beside their sections, urging on drivers and mounts, bringing every pair into draft. Jim Thomas leaned from his saddle to smack the broad rump of a wheel horse, while Barbara forged along beneath him. Two days before, when the going first became heavy, she had tried to pick her way through the mud like a lady caught in a storm in her best slippers and stockings. Now she spattered through regardless and when she slipped into a deep mud hole fairly bucked herself out of it.

There are certain men who have a way with horses and Jim Thomas was one of them. For him and his gift the battery was eternally grateful in that desperate march. When the heavy *fourgon* wagon sank deep in some muddy morass and stuck as if embedded in concrete, they sent for the Texan. He spoke to and quieted the exhausted team, standing with rolling eyes, quivering flanks, and shaking limbs. Taking the reins from the driver, he ordered him and all others away from the vicinity. Then he gathered the reins and called to the team. Out of their last reserve of strength, the horses gave him that supreme effort which swearing or whipping could not draw from them. They wrenched the wagon out of the mudhole, dragged it onward.

Alone, the gun sections made the last lap to the positions. They had to; they could not fail. They halted and unlimbered in rear of disused front-line trenches and strands of barbed wire. The artillery had arrived ahead of the infantry and between them and the Germans were only a few sentry posts. Cannoneers, sent forward to form a skirmish line against enemy patrols, stared nervously into the blackness ahead. Behind their field pieces, they were at home—ready to stand fast and serve them, though the Kaiser's gunners attempted to blast them out with counter-battery. Out here with only a few light machine guns and pistols, they were in a state of highly uncomfortable suspense.

Crouched in that dim line, a lieutenant heard a body of men approaching from the rear. Somebody stumbled over him.

"Get to blazes off of me!" he whispered fiercely.

"Gangway, then," the stumbler growled back. "This is where the marines belong."

"This is where artillery don't," responded the other. "Welcome, a thousand times welcome."

"Artillery out in front!" the marine marveled.

"Too true. I'm Lieutenant Hale. You relieving us?"

"Lieutenant Fielding, Marines. Yep, taking over."

"Thanks. The redlegs retire with a deep bow to the infantry, Queen of Battles."

"Every man to his trade," said the marine. "You do your share. Without you birds to blow up barbed wire, trenches, and pillboxes, the whole shooting match would be stalled."

"Coming from a marine, that's handsome," the artilleryman remarked. "The home newspapers said Belleau Wood was captured by the marines, 'supported by the fire of a few French field guns'—which was us."

"Stow it!" the other snapped. "That was a slip of the censor. He let the word 'marines' go through and wouldn't allow mention of Army outfits."

"No hard feelings," said the D Battery officer. "We stand by each other. So long and good luck. We'll get back to the guns."

At the artillery position, mud-plastered men were piling shells, 2500 to a battery, by their guns. Shrouded by night, muffled by rain, activity hummed around the fringe of the German lines thrust out to form the St. Mihiel salient. The greatest American army ever assembled for an attack, 400,000 men, was preparing to join battle. Grant's Army of the Potomac had numbered only 125,000 at its maximum.

Corporal Thomas, returning to the combat train on the road, looked at the luminous dial of his wrist watch. It was close to one o'clock, the hour when all the guns in the sector would open up. He groped through the dark to where he had left Barbara. Usually dependable in standing, she had strayed and he could not find her. Worried, for she might break and run when the artillery shattered the silence, he risked a shrill whistle he had been teaching her to answer. A sergeant swore at him for it, but almost at once he heard the splash of hoofs in the mud, and the mare's soft muzzle was in his hands.

It was none too soon. On the dot of one, like the crack of doom, the guns crashed in unison, swelling into a vast diapason of sound. To the infantry looking back, all the dark woods seemed suddenly ablaze. From the German lines S.O.S. rockets soared, but their batteries, smothered in high explosive, could give little succor. Hour after hour the American bombardment continued, and at five the light artillery laid down a barrage which, followed closely by the half-drowned infantry, rolled forward, every burst a geyser of mud and steel, for three hours more. American planes, masters of air this time, swooped down to machine gun the retreating foe.

The German first line was taken, then the second and third. Towns and machine-gun nests were outflanked and mopped up. Here and there the enemy stood and struck back, but not for long. He seldom paused in his rapid withdrawal from the salient.

Close after the pursuing American infantry rolled the guns. Hitherto the men at the firing batteries had not often seen their targets; they had fired by data, measured on maps, and corrections telephoned back by forward observing officers. Now, with open sights, they poured shells into garrisoned houses and saw them erupt streams of fleeing figures in field gray. For several days the batteries struggled through quagmires of yellow slime, unlimbering, firing, limbering up and pushing on again. In spite of attacks by German bombers, casualties were light. Still, the tremendous effort required of the horses told on them heavily. They were exhausted and weak for want of sufficient food, for forage supplies had not been able to keep up. Toward the last of the action, even the small bags of oats, which wise section chiefs had tucked away in caisson pockets and *fourgon* boxes, were gone, and there was nothing to feed the horses but a little hay, when an outfit was lucky enough to find a dump along the road. The animals looked like equine scarecrows when orders for relief came at last and the division countermarched to the rear.

Battery D halted for a time near a farmhouse. It was there that the Regimental Adjutant, passing in a motorcycle sidecar, beheld a soldier tying a nosebag full of oats on his mount.

"Hold up," the officer ordered his driver. "Corporal, you with the nosebag, come here. Where'd you get those oats? Has there been an issue? Heaven knows we need forage."

The soldier saluted. "No, sir. No issue. Got these from the farmhouse."

The Adjutant frowned. "You know the penalty for stealing from the French? I know your horse is half starved, but we can't stand for theft from civilians. You're under arrest. Your name and battery?"

"Corporal Thomas, Battery D. But I didn't steal the oats, sir."

"Mean to tell me the farmer gave 'em to you? Not a chance."

"I bought 'em—out of my pay. The captain can ask the farmer."

"I'll be hanged! I didn't— Well, sorry, Corporal. Nice mare you've got there." The sidecar popped off down the road.

The Adjutant was still wanting to talk about it when the regiment at last reached a rest area, with barracks for the men and fine stables for the horses. He had his chance at mess that night.

"This corporal in D Battery I ran into—he'd been buying oats for his horse out of his own pay, believe it or not," the Adjutant held forth. "Must have been doing it every chance he got since we pulled out of the salient. His mount looked sleek and well-fed. Best-looking nag in any outfit. Seemed as if I'd seen her before. Neat little chestnut mare."

"Probably the mare young Brent used to ride back in the States," said Colonel Mack. "I'd heard she had rejoined. Just how I don't know—officially."

"Quite a jumper, isn't she?" one of the majors interjected. "She's got a reputation through the whole regiment."

"If she gets through the war," the Colonel remarked, "she may become a regimental tradition. Like 'Putnam' in Reilly's battery."

Persuaded by the young officers, the old campaigner told the story of the horse he had known when he served as second lieutenant during the Boxer Rebellion in China—how when the American contingent, with the Allies, was marching to the relief of the desperately besieged Legations in Pekin, one of Reilly's gun sections started to climb a steep bank to take position to fire. Almost to the top, trace springs had snapped under the strain, and only Putnam, the near wheel horse, remained in draft. That veteran, sturdy shoulders hard against his collar, mighty haunch muscles flexed and standing out, alone held the gun and limber on the slope, saving them from a crash; then hauled them up on the high ground. He served through the campaign and seven years later was retired and pensioned in a pasture. When the old hero died, he was given a regular military funeral—flag-draped caisson, firing squad, and all—probably the only war horse ever so honored.

The Lieutenant Colonel told of Jumbo of the First Field Artillery, a veritable top sergeant of a horse. He used to keep every recruit horse in his battery in order;

if he caught one balking, he would sink his teeth in its neck and shake till the loafer worked. Every nag in the corral always granted Jumbo precedence when the stable doors were opened, and no soldier dared feed another horse sugar in his presence. So heavy were his neck muscles, a special collar had to be made for him. A hater of rattlesnakes, he stamped every one he saw to death and attempted to do for Oklahoma what St. Patrick did for Ireland.

The senior major remembered Foxhall of the Third Field. A great bucker, never ridden bareback, Foxhall was a fine worker in harness. He was also considerable of a joker. In the Spanish War when the horses were lowered over the side of the transport to swim a short distance to the Cuban shore, Foxhall elected to swim five miles out to sea, hotly pursued by a boatload of indignant sailors. Grown old, he was assigned to the battery bread cart, which he hauled undriven every morning to the bakery, where he received a loaf as his pay. He lived to the age of forty, when he died of pneumonia.

But the most famous horse of the Third was Rodney, the other major reminded the mess. Rodney and his teammate Shaw pulled not only their own but other guns out of the Cuban mud and brought them into action. Rodney, like Jumbo, hazed rookie horses till they made friends, after which he treated them with dignified consideration. Left at Fort Myer in his old age, when his battery went on a hike, he was condemned and ordered sold by an inspector who did not know his history. Rodney's soldier friends returned to find him up at auction. When they tried to buy him, a mean-spirited dealer bid up the price, but the battery, digging down into its pockets, recaptured him for $120. Petted, groomed, fed all he could safely eat, a favorite with all, the grand old horse lived till he was thirty.

As the last speaker finished, a quiet voice addressed the Regimental Commander.

"*Mon Colonel*, may I venture to add something?"

It was the French *liaison* officer attached to the regiment. His jet black hair was grayed at the temples; his features finely chiseled and mobile. Medal ribbons gleamed on the breast of his horizon-blue tunic, its sleeves bearing the *galons* of a captain, and wound and service chevrons.

"Certainly, De Condenbove," Colonel Mack answered. "We Americans have been monopolizing this. You of the French artillery surely have heroic tales of your horses. Tell us some."

"This, sir, is not a story," the Frenchman went on in his perfect English. "It is something I have myself written. Forgive me if I presume."

The mess listened attentively, as the officer, liked and respected throughout the regiment, drew a paper from his pocket and read:

"THE ARTILLERY HORSE'S PRAYER"

"To thee, my master, I offer my prayer.

"Treat me as a living being, not as a machine.

"Feed me, water and care for me, and when the day's work is done, groom me carefully so that my circulation may act well, for remember: a good grooming is equivalent to half a feed. Clean my feet and legs and keep them in good condition, for they are the most important parts of my body.

"Pet me sometimes, be always gentle to me so that I may serve you the more gladly and learn to love you.

"Do not jerk the reins, do not whip me when I am going uphill. Do not force me out of the regular gait or you will not have my strength when you want it. Never strike, beat or kick me when I do not understand what you mean, but give me a chance to understand you. Watch me, and if I fail to do your bidding, see if something is not wrong with my harness or feet.

"Don't draw the straps too tight: give me freedom to move my head. Don't make my load too heavy, and oh! I pray thee, have me well shod every month.

"Examine my teeth when I do not eat; I may have some teeth too long or I may have an ulcerated tooth and that, you know, is very painful. Do not tie my head in an unnatural position or take away my best defense against flies and mosquitoes by cutting off my tail.

"I cannot, alas, tell you when I am thirsty, so give me pure cold water frequently. Do all you can to protect me from the sun; and throw a cover over me—not when I am working, but when I am standing in the cold.

"I always try to do cheerfully the work you require of me. And day and night I stand for hours patiently waiting for you.

"In this war, like any other soldier, I will do my best without hope of any war-cross, content to serve my country and you, and, if need be, I will die calm and dignified on the battlefield; therefore, oh! my master, treat me in the kindest way and your God will reward you here and hereafter.

"I am not irreverent if I ask this, my prayer, in the name of Him who was born in a stable."

Colonel Mack stirred in his chair and broke the succeeding silence.

"Amen to that, Captain," he said, "and our sincere thanks for a beautiful and a touching tribute." The mess warmly seconded him. A far-away look in his eyes, the Colonel spoke on:

"We get fond of our horses, of those friends of ours," he quietly observed. "Too fond, I sometimes think, for the peace of our hearts. We've got to see them hit by shell fragments—and maybe put them out of their agony with a bullet through their heads. We've got to work them nearly to death—and we all know they're willing to give us all they've got—to work them until they're reduced to the state ours are in now. When their service is over, it's only a few of them we can pension and let live out their days in green pastures. But we can take decent care of them while they're with us. And we can honor them."

The old artilleryman lifted his glass. Then he gave his toast.

"Gentlemen, to those that keep the caissons rolling along—our horses!"

They drank it standing.

" She's yours now corporal ".

10: NOBLESSE OBLIGE

Lightly answered the Colonel's son: "I hold by the blood of my clan:
Take up the mare for my father's gift—by God, she has carried a man!"
The red mare ran to the Colonel's son, and nuzzled against his breast;
"We be two strong men," said Kamal then, "but she loveth the younger best."

KIPLING: The Ballad of East and West

JUST before the Colonel proposed his toast, a young officer, haggard and pale, had entered the mess unnoticed. Hastily he filled a wine glass and drank the toast with fervor. When the glasses were lowered, the others saw him.

"Brent!" boomed the Colonel amid a chorus of welcome. "Glad to have you back! Are you all right now? You look pretty dragged out still."

"All right, sir, thank you," the newcomer answered in a voice still hoarse from gas. "I had to hurry back soon as they'd let me loose from the hospital. I was afraid they might shift me to another regiment."

They drank his health and gave him the news of the regiment, especially of the recovery of Barbara. Brent, on duty with the firing battery after the first phase of Soissons, had not learned that Thomas had recaptured the mare; shortly afterwards he had been gassed and sent to the hospital. Now, answering his eager questions, they told him of the mare's adventures. She was in fine shape, they assured him, and could not have had better care than that Caisson Corporal in his battery had given her. While the French *liaison* officer winked, they spun the yarn of the trick with the French general's charger, which had saved Barbara from the hazard of an inspection. They related the exploits of Thomas and the mare in the mud of St. Mihiel. Then they packed the convalescent off to his billet.

Brent did not turn in at once. For a long time he sat on the edge of his bed in deep thought. Should he take back the mare, he pondered. It had been Thomas who had recovered her, but that was just a fluke. Events at the camp in Virginia flooded back through his memory. That man Thomas had been downright insubordinate. He remembered the baleful, murderous look the fellow had given him. In this war, he had heard, officers had been shot by soldiers who hated them and the killing laid to the enemy. While he could not bring himself to believe that Thomas was that kind, wouldn't it be thought that he, Johnny Brent, was yellow if he relinquished the mare to the other? He shook his head angrily.

How did the other officers feel? He had not wanted to ask; after all it was *his* party. They seemed to assume that Barbara was his mount, and what rights did an enlisted man have in such a matter? There was sentiment, of course, that, *noblesse oblige*, he ought to be decently appreciative of the corporal's services. If a soldier souvenired a German Lueger pistol or a *Gott Mit Uns* belt buckle for you, you passed over enough francs for him to stake himself in a crap game or get several skinfuls of red ink. But imagine offering that man Thomas money for Barbara! Brent had a strong notion it would be thrown in his face. Still, there were other favors that could be done.

The old romantic tales he had grown up on invaded Johnny Brent's harassed mind. Forsooth it would be a knightly deed and one full chivalrous to give Barbara back to Thomas. Bah! What chivalry was there in a war where they used gas?

Certainly Thomas was fond of the mare—just as he, Johnny Brent, was. And Barbara was fond of both of them, though probably she knew the Texan better, since he had been with her more. But her lot as an officer's mount would be easier. How proud he had been of her that day he had ridden her in the parade in Washington!

His head was splitting when at last he got to his feet. This affair had best be settled here and now. Brent called downstairs for his striker and sent him off with orders for Corporal Thomas to report at once.

The summons hit Jim Thomas like a blow in the pit of the stomach. So it had come, after all. He had been a fool not to expect it and get set for it. That's what you got for believing rumors, for taking it for granted that Brent had been sent back to the States. Wild, crazy ideas raced through his brain—of deserting with Barbara—of challenging the Lieutenant to fight for her and let the better man keep her. He pulled himself back to reason. What rot he had been thinking! How in blazes could you desert on horseback in France? Imagine socking a guy just back from the hospital!

The soldier who stepped through the doorway into Brent's billet was outwardly impassive and military. He said: "Sir, Corporal Thomas reports as ordered."

"Sit down, Corporal," invited the pale officer with sunken cheeks.

Thomas, ignoring the invitation, remained standing.

"I want to thank you for what you've done for Barbara," Brent said warmly. He did not seem to notice that Thomas's lips curled. "Never thought we'd see her again," he went on. He stared into space, remembering. "When you spotted her passing us in that charge and then I heard the Boche machine guns open up, I was sure she was gone for good. She must have had some other tough times, too, since we lost her in the States."

"She did," Thomas declared grimly. "You ought to have seen her mouth and her flanks. But she's got over it. She knows me again. She—" He fell abruptly silent.

"I told you once Barbara was an officer's mount," Brent resumed quietly. "She is. No officer could ask a finer."

Jim Thomas bowed to the inevitable. He spoke with difficulty. "Whenever the lieutenant's ready to ride her again—"

"The lieutenant won't be," Johnny Brent interrupted with a smile. "Not while you're with the outfit. She's yours now, Corporal. I won't rank you out of her nor will any other man, if I can help it."

Jim Thomas tried to thank him and stopped. His voice seemed a bit unsteady. At last he managed it lamely, saluted and started to leave. At the doorway he turned, stepped back and extended his hand.

"Sir," he asked, "will the lieutenant shake?"

He had his answer quickly.

"He sure will, Corporal. Put her there."

"Condemn that horse,
break that corporal"

11: THE STORMING OF BLANC MONT

*They are firing, we are falling, and the red skies rend and
    shiver us.
    Barbara, Barbara, we may not loose a breath—
Be at the bursting doors of doom, and in the dark deliver us,
    Who loosen the last window on the sun of sudden death.*
                        CHESTERTON: *Ballad of Saint Barbara*

THE night the toast to the horses was drunk was the
Colonel's last night with the regiment he had organized.

Orders promoting and transferring him to command the Field Artillery Brigade of a National Guard Division were swiftly complied with, not only because they were peremptory but because haste made it easier for him to say farewell. For him no new command ever could fill the place in his heart held by this regiment he had created, imbued with *esprit de corps* and led into battle.

To replace him arrived a lean, sour-faced officer. Colonel Mack had been a disciplinarian; this new C.O. was a martinet. His attitude clearly was: This lax, rugged outfit is due for a reformation, renaissance, and all-around hell-raising and I'm going to see that it gets it. Promptly he ordered a regimental review.

Passing before him, men, guns, and equipment presented a trim appearance, but the horses had not yet had time to recover. Gaunt and mangy, they resembled Napoleon's worn gun teams in the earlier stages of the retreat from Moscow. The Colonel frowned, clicked his tongue, and muttered. Fresh from staff duty, the mud of St. Mihiel was only hearsay to him. But with the passing of D Battery he exhibited sudden interest.

At least there was one animal in this outfit which looked fit for a better destiny than the Sign of the Golden Horsehead, that emblem of the butcher shops where the French sold horse meat to an unfinical populace. A neat little mare, the Colonel pronounced. Good conformation and gait, well-fed, and not a sign of mange.

Barbara was aware that she was being admired. The eternal feminine responded. It could properly be said (in view of the word's derivation) that she bridled. Head up, too obviously oblivious of the attention she was drawing, she tripped along for all the world like a handsome lass delighting in but pretending not to notice the flattering stares of a group of lads. Jim Thomas, sensing the cause of his mount's byplay, struggled to suppress a grin. Neither he nor Barbara reflected that pride goeth before a fall.

"Adjutant," called the Colonel's harsh voice, "see that chestnut mare there. Best-looking horse in the whole outfit. Only decent one."

The Adjutant had been admiring also. He was about to explain the reason for Barbara's superior condition— to tell of the attachment between her and her rider. But he thought fast (which was why he was Adjutant), and all he said was, "Yes, sir. She makes a good appearance."

The Colonel came out with it.

"I'll take her for my mount," he decreed. "Have her sent to Headquarters."

Now the Colonel, with an automobile assigned to carry him over the fine roads of France, had little or no need of a horse. That, the Adjutant realized, would be neither here nor there. No more would the fact that other mounts were available, nor the truth of Barbara's history. Such circumstances would not weigh with a narrow, arbitrary, strictly military mind.

"The Colonel would be ill-advised to take that mare," the Adjutant lied fluently. "She's a new replacement. Didn't go through the last show that wore down the rest of our nags. That's why she looks well. The trouble is she's broken-winded, and I understand she'll have to be condemned."

The Colonel turned on him a sceptical gaze from fishy eyes.

"Broken-winded, you say? Humph. I'll see about that."

Then the Lieutenant Colonel came to the rescue.

"Thinking of using that mare, sir?" he asked. "Thought of taking her over myself a while ago. Probably her wind is good enough for all we'd require of her. What warned me off was seeing her stumble. Can't abide an animal that falls over its own feet."

Looking only slightly less suspicious, the Colonel gruffly ordered, "Get that mare over here at once."

The Adjutant walked back to an orderly.

"Have Corporal Thomas, Battery D, report mounted to the Commanding Officer at once." He lowered his voice. "Just before he gets here, tell him to have his mare stumble."

"Sir?" The orderly gaped.

"Hang it, man!" the Adjutant whispered fiercely. "You heard me. Deliver that order word for word. Double-time!"

Would Thomas understand that strange order and obey it? The Adjutant waited in considerable trepidation. He and the Lieutenant Colonel were running a risk that might have serious consequences if they, officers and gentlemen, were caught in a deliberate lie to their commander—particularly to this one. Visions of court martial charges, of disgrace at the reclassification depot for officers at Blois, chased through the nervous Adjutant's mind. Why had they acted as they had on the spur of the moment? The loyalty of the regiment to its own against an outsider. The fact that the little chestnut mare had, in a way, become the regimental mascot. Those were reasons enough. Yet a court would hardly accept them as favorable evidence.

Barbara never understood the happenings of the next few minutes. She was turned out of the column bound for the stables and cantered hastily toward a knot of officers, and suddenly the beloved man on her back, splendid rider though he was, attempted to make her change leads in the clumsiest fashion imaginable. At the time she felt such a jerk of bit and bite of spur as she had not know since those cruel days when the shell-shocked Frenchman rode her. Small wonder that in consternation and pain she stumbled. It was even more surprising when the ex-cowboy in her saddle pitched over her head and sprawled in front of his Colonel.

Thomas had managed it skillfully, and the officers had partially distracted the Colonel. Now he surveyed the scene with a look of disgust and barked:

"Have that horse condemned. Break this corporal and send him back to equitation school."

The Colonel did not last long enough with the regiment to see either order enforced. Kind Providence removed him to some other suffering command. Had the stratagem of the stumbling not succeeded, he was perfectly capable of having taken Barbara with him when he went. As it was, he left alone. There were merry celebrations at the messes after his going. The Adjutant brought out his guitar and, speeding the departed Colonel, rendered the song of the Mounted Service School at Fort Reilly, to the riotous and disrespectful mirth of his audience.

> Then I was given a draft horse,
>   Schooled in the West Riding Hall;
> Splendid four-gaiter they called him—
>   A walk, trot, stumble, and fall. . . .

When the regiment had orders for the Front again, it marched under its able and respected Lieutenant Colonel.

Rest had been all too brief. The division paid the

penalty of the fame it had won as shock troops of reckless gallantry. As part of a French Corps, it was to assault Blanc Mont, German stronghold since 1914, key to all the battle line in the Champagne between Rheims and the Argonne.

By train, then by road, the division moved forward, on through the desolation of a sector which had been won and lost and won again in some of the fiercest fighting of the war. Past smashed trenches scarring the chalk-white soil, rusty mazes of barbed wire, countless shell craters, heaps of stone that once had been homes. No tree, not even a blade of grass relieved the utter devastation. Here were strewn huddled heaps of horizon blue and field gray, still unburied Frenchmen and Germans, rotting in the sun. They were many. Not even hardened veterans could pass them and the motionless forms of horses and shattered cannon without uncomfortable premonition. Ahead surely lay another field of Armageddon like unto this one they were crossing. They threw off the foreboding with the soldier's fatalism. If a bullet or a shell came along with your number on it, that was that. Meanwhile, what was the use of worrying?

Again the batteries marched under the cloak of night, down a broad road to the front. The well-trained teams, scarcely needing guidance, kept to the right, with the proper interval between carriages. Once the leading section of the combat train of D Battery walked out to close up. After some time Stable Sergeant Quinn, riding at its head, peered through the gloom intently. There was something peculiar about the gait of the animal drawing the vehicle ahead. Not only that; its ears were too long and they flopped. It was no horse, but a mule. The artillery caissons were about to follow a machine gun-section into the front line. Quinn's timely discovery turned them back, and they found the side road on which they should have turned off and rejoined the battery.

The artillery opened with an intense bombardment and laid down a rolling barrage. Preceded by the bursting shells and most welcome tanks, the infantry attacked. A hot fire from the German lines girding the stronghold poured into them. Stubbornly they drove through, overrunning the enemy trenches, never faltering in spite of staggering losses. The field guns, reaching the limit of their range, limbered up and followed.

Only the aviators can survey a great modern battle as generals used to from a near-by hilltop, and the aviators, usually forced to fly high, are limited to a distant prospect. As for the troops on the ground, each soldier sees only his own little segment of the combat.

For Lieutenant John Brent, the storming of Blanc Mont and its formidable defenses was a drama of blood and thunder played on the small stage of his own immediate surroundings, and much of it was enacted behind a succession of curtains, the crests over which his battery fired. Commanding his four guns, he seemed to himself like an orchestra leader. Again and again his right arm swept up and down, and the 75's cracked and flamed, their barrels gliding back in recoil, then returning into battery. Breeches clicked open and shell cases clanged musically on the trails. New projectiles were snapped in, gunners bent over their sights. Lanyards jerked and four more shells screeched on their way over the crest toward the invisible target. Teams trotted up to drag the cannon forward. The next crest loomed in front, like another lowered curtain.

At intervals, Brent and his men at the guns no longer were a tiny, isolated group in this mighty theater of life and death but suddenly stepped upon the stage themselves. Once, in a respite, a rolling kitchen managed to reach them, and fifty hungry men were clustering about it for slum and coffee. It was then a German shell struck in the center of the position, only a few yards away. Tied to a wheel of the kitchen stood a horse, between the explosion and the men. Because the poor animal took the full force of the blast, the men lived. Then there came a desperate moment when a plane with ominous black crosses on its wings swooped down out of the sky and dived at the battery, its machine guns blazing. The artillerymen knew sheer terror, a dreadful defenselessness, their ears ringing with the roar of motors and the vicious singing of bullets. An instant and the plane was gone. Most, but not all, of the figures clinging to the earth rose. The gun squads staggered back to their pieces. Again the executive's arm rose and fell, and the symphony of volleys crashed. The battery was still in action.

Brent felt the wild rhythm, the fierce joy of combat, as hour on hour the grimy cannoneers served the smoke-wreathed guns. A stirring phrase ran through his head:

And their batteries, black with battle. . . .

Something by that English poet Chesterton, wasn't it? How did it go?

The touch and the tornado; all our guns give tongue together,
  St. Barbara for the gunnery and God defend the right,
  They are stopped and gapped and battered as we blast
away. . . .

The diminishing piles of shells beside the guns called back Brent's thoughts. More ammunition! Where was the combat train? Ah, there it came up the road which German shellfire was beginning to sweep. They had almost made it when a black geyser erupted to the left of the trotting column. Above the reverberation soared the shrill, agonized scream of a horse, mortally wounded. A shell fragment had hit the near-lead of the first section. The driver, unhurt, struggled clear, shot the kicking animal, and stripped off the harness.

Brent saw Corporal Thomas trot up, quickly unsaddle Barbara, and harness her in the dead horse's place. That was the duty of a caisson corporal in such an event, and the single mounts of the regiment had been trained to work in harness for just such an emergency. But, Brent realized, it must have come hard. He heard the driver, a Milwaukee lad of German parentage, call to Thomas as he mounted up:

"Tough, Jim. But I'll take good care of her."

The caissons rolled up, their precious ammunition was unloaded and they disappeared down the road for more.

German batteries had the range of the road to the metre and they knew it must now be in use for vital ammunition supply. They made a giant's bowling alley of it, an alley thunderous with a rolling barrage of high explosive. Still the combat train came dashing through, drivers bent low over the necks of the racing teams, caissons clattering and bouncing, as the column veered out into a field to avoid a particularly deadly stretch of the road, then back on it again. Twice more, miraculously, they made that perilous trip without disaster.

But the 75's were insatiable. They ate up ammunition at six rounds a minute per gun. The fire so desperately needed by the attacking infantry must not cease. Soon an anxious frown creased Lieutenant Brent's brow again. In the tumult he shouted over his shoulder:

Driverless, they wheeled about

Paul Brown
42

"Any sign of that combat train yet, Thomas?"

"Not yet, sir," the corporal answered. "Wait—yes—there they are!"

The van of the train was emerging from behind a clump of trees screening a turn of the road—ready for a dash to the guns. Thomas recognized Barbara, still in the lead pair of the first section.

The German guns were now mixing shrapnel with the high explosive, white smoke clouds mingling with the gray-black bursts. The shrapnel balls rattled on the hard surface of the road like hailstones.

At the firing battery, Brent and Thomas, safe behind the crest in so-called dead space, watched the advancing train with mounting apprehension.

The first section was out from behind the trees when a high shrapnel burst caught it. A sergeant and his mount went down as if struck by a lightning bolt. The boy from Milwaukee on Barbara's back threw up his arms, swayed and fell. Behind him the saddles of the swing and wheel pairs were suddenly empty, too. The horses of the leading team were still on their feet, but, driverless, they recoiled in a rearing, tangled mass on their limber.

Groaning in anguish, Brent turned to the man who had been standing at his side. Thomas was no longer there. At top speed, he was running down the shell-swept road.

Futile bravery, thought Brent. Thomas could not

reach that milling team in time. There was a far better chance for men from the rear of the train, if they were unhit, to rush up and halt the threatened runaway.

But Thomas had stopped part way down the road. His shrill whistle cut through the bass detonations of the shells. Out of the confusion in front of the limber a chestnut hide emerged. Ears on a well-shaped Arab head pricked up. . . .

There is a tale told of the manner in which the Prophet Mohammed established his celebrated stud of the Arab blood—how he took forty mares, trained in the art of warfare, and shut them in a stable without food or water for two days. Only when the hoofs of the ravenous animals almost had battered down the walls were the doors opened. Out dashed the herd in a furious gallop toward the river. When they nearly had reached the bank, Mohammed caused war trumpets to be sounded from the opposite direction. Thirty-five of the mares plunged on to drink, but five, in spite of their terrible thirst, turned back and obeyed the rallying call of the trumpets. It was from those five that the Prophet bred the renowned steeds that carried the Sword of Islam on its path of conquest.

So, likewise, Barbara heard and obeyed. She struggled forward, dragging the rest of the team into line. Down the road into the inferno of hurtling steel rolled the driverless section. Thomas, running back to the firing battery, heard a faint cheer and knew that the rest of the train was following. On it came at a dead gallop, through a rain of shells which seemed to burst at the very feet of the foaming teams. Caissons, skirting craters, tilted crazily, righted themselves. Barbara and her team-mates swerved at the blast of each concussion, but galloped on.

Now the men at the battery could see the whites of the rolling eyes of the onrushing horses. The road led through the guns and over the crest. Would the frantic team check its headlong pace or charge straight through? Cannoneers left their posts to form a barrier line to hold to the last moment. They flung up their hands, waved their helmets and yelled.

It worked—that and long training. Hundreds of times the teams of the combat train had galloped up to the guns, wheeled about in their rear and halted. Again, though driverless, they followed the familiar routine, executing the evolution neatly, with the rest of the train behind them, and standing with trembling legs and heaving flanks. Men hurried to their heads, while other hands unlatched caisson doors and pulled out the precious ammunition. Jim Thomas, his arm around Barbara's neck, rubbed her ears and whispered into them words that none but she could hear in the encompassing din.

The tide of battle rose, lifted to a tumultuous crescendo for the bloody capture of the ridge, ebbed slowly. Contesting each foot of ground, savagely counter-attacking, the enemy withdrew. Beyond the Aisne River he would halt and hold. But not for long. The stage was set now for the grim finale of the Argonne Forest and the climax which men hopefully called a lasting peace.

During the latter part of the Battle of Blanc Mont, the division's infantry, its ranks thinned by heavy casualties, was relieved. Its artillery, however, remained in line in support of the fresh division whose artillery was not yet trained. Gradually drumfire sank to sporadic bombardments. Days seemed comparatively peaceful, and worn men could snatch sleep nights, in spite of crimson flares and explosions marking the destruction of towns by the retreating Germans. Only when the victors pressed the pursuit too closely did the vanquished sullenly retaliate.

Jim Thomas, cited and promoted to a sergeantcy, had found another horse to replace Barbara in the team. At dusk on the last day of the battle he was riding her through a field with a message for Headquarters. Four miles away a battery of Austrian 88's, about to limber up and continue its retreat, fired a last salvo. The shells from those guns of high muzzle velocity, giving no shrieking warning of their approach, flashed and cracked in the field like whip-lashes amplified a thousandfold.

The chestnut mare jumped convulsively and shuddered. The man on her back reeled and slumped in his saddle. His body slid to the ground and lay still.

She knows the still figure.

12: FORTUNES OF WAR

*And, faith, ye shall never fail us when the whimpering bullets
    fly,*
*When the lances shiver and splinter and Death in his spurs
    goes by:*
*When the stricken reels in his saddle and the chill hand drops
    the rein,*
And bloody out of the battle ye wheel to the tents again!

W. H. OGILVIE: *Remounts*

DUSK deepened into night, and the stars came out.
Though guns still grumbled in the distance, a comparative silence settled on the lonely field. Along the road

at its western edge, reinforcements and supply trucks streamed toward the front.

That French field, dotted with the bodies of men and horses bore a certain resemblance to another battleground in American history. On the prairie grass of the Little Big Horn, forty years before, lay Custer, his officers, and his troopers, killed by the Sioux. And then, as now, alone among the still forms stood a badly wounded horse, legs braced, head drooping.

Like Comanche, the mount of slain Captain Myles Keogh and the only survivor of Custer's force except the Indian scout Curly, Barbara would not desert her master. Never stirring from his side, at intervals she nosed the still figure of Sergeant Thomas, then lifted her head to gaze piteously around her. On the road, the shadowy column never ceased its forward flow, slowing only as it gave way to the right to make room for laden ambulances and empty trucks, bound for the rear.

An hour passed. Over on the road the motor of an ambulance sputtered and died. A weary driver and his helper got assistance to shove the vehicle out of the traffic into the field. The driver lifted the hood and began fumbling in the darkness. His helper, leaning against a wheel, encouraged the driver to sulphurous mutterings.

"Wish you had a flashlight, huh?" the helper retorted to the driver's fervent expression of a desire. "Sure, that'd be grand. Course we could send a wireless message to a

Boche bomber, but a light would be cheaper and just as good. 'Bout time you knew the touch system of motor repair."

The driver blasted him with magnificent fluency. Grinning, the helper egged him on:

"We got some wounded in this bus might like to get back to the hospital some time tonight. Me now, I'm in no hurry. I like to watch you work, Tinker Bell."

The driver branded him as the supreme mistake of a long and dim-witted line and ordered him to turn on the ignition and crank up. When the other obliged, the engine showed a few signs of life, then expired again.

"If at first you don't succeed," the helper blithely remarked, "Try, try— Say, something moved over in the field!"

"Yeh?" the driver snapped. "Go ahead. Tell me a ghost story to pass the time."

"No kidding. I saw it. Something big."

"It's the wolf, Little Red Riding Hood. Be yourself, stupid. We cleared out that field yesterday. There's nothing left there but stiffs."

"Just the same, I'm going to look see," said the helper.

"My hero!" the driver snorted from under the hood.

The investigator was soon back from the field. "I was right as usual," he announced. "What it was was a horse standing over a guy pretty badly hit but still alive. We got room on the floor of this chariot. Come on, freeze onto the other end of this stretcher."

They bandaged the unconscious Jim Thomas and gently placed him in the ambulance. The driver returned to his motor and this time succeeded in starting it. The ambulance men climbed to the seat and watched their chance to swing into the traffic. Beside them in the field a dark shape loomed.

"Hey!" said the helper. "It's the horse. Followed us over and wants to come along. Poor nag's wounded, too. Maybe we better shoot it."

"Government property," the driver reminded him. "You'd find that horse on the payroll."

"Might at that," the helper agreed. "You're right for once. Kinda touchin' sight, though. Nice little nag. Used to have a pony when I was a kid. Well, drive on, James, and don't spare the horses."

The ambulance lurched forward. Barbara stiffly moved along at its side in a limping, halting trot.

"Hey!" growled the driver. "That goat's still with us."

"Can I help it?" snapped his helper.

"It was you seen that animule first. Lean out and shoo it away. This don't look right. We ain't no horse marines."

The other swung out on the running board. "Beat it, little hoss," he called.

Barbara eyed him but kept on. She knew her master was in that ambulance and she was going to stay close to him. The helper waved an arm and yelled, "Go home, you! Go on home!"

Barbara shied away but trotted back by the car.

"Home!" the driver sniffed sarcastically. "Whaddye-mean, home? That hoss ain't got no more chance of going home than you or me has."

" 'Home,' " quoted the helper sentimentally, " 'is where the heart is.' "

"Nuts!" grunted the driver and began to sing, "When this cruel war is over—"

"Shut up, you!" his companion ordered him fiercely. "This is beginning to get to me. Speed up, can't yuh?"

Traffic had been moving faster, and there was an empty stretch ahead. The driver stepped on the accelerator.

Barbara trotted more rapidly, tried desperately to break into a gallop. She could not manage it, for the wound in her shoulder, stiffening, galled every step. Gradually she dropped back. As she saw the car receding in the darkness, she whinnied forlornly. Inside the ambulance, a wounded man groaned as if in answer.

The helper craned out to look back.

"That hoss still coming?" asked the driver.

"Guess not. Can't see it any more."

They drove on for five minutes without speaking.

"Gosh!" said the helper softly. "I thought this war had made me hardboiled."

"Forget it!" the ambulance driver snorted. "It's only a hoss, ain't it? It's going to kick in soon, too. You seen thousands of 'em fertilizing France, to say nothing of men."

"I know but—"

"Aw, fergit it," finished the driver.

Forgotten, unregarded by the streams of traffic rolling by, Barbara stood listlessly by the roadside, waiting with the long patience of dumb animals, weak and weary unto death. In the early days of the war, when the Germans drove fiercely at Paris, horses in her condition would have been shot or left to die. Later they fared little better, until the supply began to dwindle dangerously. In the summer of 1918, the average life of an artillery horse at the Front was only ten days. The imperative necessity of conserving resources forced action which humanitarian motives, perforce submerged in war, could not achieve. The war was taking that ghastly toll of draft animals which finally would reach the stupendous total of eight million.

Because it had been realized that the war horse was a means to victory, because without him the guns would stand stalled, still and impotent, rescue came to the wounded chestnut mare that night.

Through the backwash of the battle moved mobile veterinary sections, collecting incapacitated animals. One of them found Barbara in the gray of the dawn. The gray-haired lieutenant in command began to examine her.

"Hello!" he exclaimed. "It's that little mare out of D Battery. Looks like she's got a shell splinter in this shoulder. Hand me that iodine swab . . . now that instrument . . . hold her tight."

Barbara winced and trembled as he probed.

"Can't get it. Too deep," said the Vet. "Gauze now and I'll plug up this hole . . . bandages . . . good. She's lost a lot of blood, but maybe she'll be all right. Walk her around a bit."

A soldier led Barbara up and down. She walked very lamely, but she did not totter.

"Good. Guess she can make the railhead," the Vet decided. "Ticket her."

"Too bad she won't be coming back to us," the soldier mourned. "The whole regiment'll miss this here little mare. Now when horses get well, the Remount just reissues 'em regardless, instead of sending 'em back to their own outfits like they used to, don't they, Lieutenant?"

"Sure, but this case is different. This is an officer's personal mount."

"She is? Say, I never knew that before, Lieutenant."

"Now you know," pronounced the Vet decisively. "Ticket her that way."

"Yessir. You betcha." The soldier grinned.

Barbara was loaded into a train bound for one of the now numerous horse hospitals, some of them with a capacity for as many as three thousand animals. Tens of thousands of horses and mules were being cared for in hospitals in France alone. Some treated mange cases exclusively.

Others had wards for ophthalmia—partial blindness—or for hoof ailments or gas cases, while others were chiefly surgical.

Feeble and stiff, the little mare was detrained directly onto a truck and carried to the hospital. Led into a room with white walls, she was gently compelled to lie down on a covered mat. An understanding man in a white gown quietly persisted in keeping a cone over her muzzle until, breathing deep of a strange, sweetish smell, she lapsed into unconsciousness.

The mare woke, sick, dazed and bewildered by her strange surroundings. Her nostrils quivered. A stable smell gave her slight reassurance; yet it was too strongly tinged with the pungence of antiseptics to seem natural. Then, as she moved her legs, she was gripped with panic. She could find no footing. She was floating in the air. A human, regaining consciousness under such circumstances, might have imagined that he had died and was flying through some celestial realm. Barbara seemed to be soaring like a winged horse. It was exactly like the moment when, galloping at a fence with Jim Thomas on her back, she sprang into the air for one of her long, graceful leaps. She braced her shoulders—how the right one pained!— and gathered her haunches to land. But she never felt the expected shock. To her consternation, she could not alight from this jump.

Gradually she came to understand. Around her belly

Paul Brown

" That goat's still with us "

was one of those broad webbing slings, such as had been used when she was embarked in and debarked from the transport. (This was to keep her weight off her forelegs and spare her wounded shoulder.) She finally discovered that her hind legs could touch the floor.

Watered, fed and groomed, Barbara grew accustomed to this peculiar state of affairs. Although she dreaded the visits of the white-clad man who came to dress her wound, she sensed that he hurt her no more than he could help. From the way he talked to her and handled her, clearly he was a friend.

Her wound healed rapidly. Curiously, it left a right-angle scar, apex down, resembling the chevron a wounded soldier was entitled to wear on the right sleeve of his uniform.

The day came when she was led slowly around a covered exercise track, walked a little longer each time. But she continued to limp badly. The orderly leading her watched her doubtfully and sadly, wondering whether this fine little animal was lamed for life.

Then wrath from the skies descended on the big horse hospital. It was not the actual objective of the German bombing squadron that hummed over it with roaring motors. The big planes, returning from a raid on a rail-head, simply were paying their compliments in passing to the dark mass of buildings below, dropping the few bombs remaining in their racks. Yet none of the hospital staff cowering beneath knew they were only a casual and hap-hazard target. There is something dreadfully personal about an air raid. Like primitive men caught without shelter in a thunderstorm and believing themselves doomed of the gods, the victims waited dumbly to be blasted into eternity.

A menacing buzzing as of gigantic, angry hornets. Whistling swoops and tremendous, shattering crashes. In her stall, Barbara tugged wildly at her halter shank. This was a hundredfold worse than the muffled crashes of the depth bombs that had shaken her in the hold of the transport—worse than shell fire in the heat of battle. Yet the little mare, veteran that she was, did not give way to complete panic. Hers was not the abject terror of the poor beasts in the stalls on either side of her. They were shell-shock patients, and now, groaning and trembling, their plight was pitiful.

Another crash, and the wooden headquarters building flamed crimson against the night. Sirens shrieked. A gallant fire detail dragged themselves out from under cover and ran for the apparatus. Unhampered by bombers now winging back to Germany, the firemen fought to save the stables. There were farm boys in that detail who had seen barns burn, who had heard the piteous lowing of suffocating cattle and the terrible screams of imprisoned horses when the flames reached them. They fought like demons and at last, blackened and scorched, extinguished the blaze that threatened to spread.

It was more fortunate than they realized that the hospital had been saved, for the next day heavy animal casualties from the Argonne were shipped in, and the place was packed and jammed. Harried veterinarians, resorting to every expedient to make room, called in remount inspectors. Here and there horses were led out and hastily examined. Some were returned to their stalls, others motioned to be added to the column, bound for the village.

One of the latter was Barbara.

☆ ☆ ☆ ☆ ☆ ☆ ☆ ☆

The hospital was still busy and crowded on a certain day early in November, when a racket—wild shouting, blowing of bugles, and shooting—started in the village. Swiftly it spread, and soon every member of the Veterinary Corps on duty at the hospital was joining in a tumultuous celebration. Puzzled, a little apprehensive, the horses in the corrals stood with pricked-up ears, wondering what it was all about. Could they have understood that this was Armistice Day, surcease from the agony of four long years of war, the four-footed creatures would have rejoiced, too.

"*Fini la guerre!*" the village screamed and shouted again and again. Down at the station, a train puffed in, whistling in jubilation. A sergeant of American artillery, pale and thin, his left sleeve hanging empty, stepped out of a compartment into the midst of the uproar. Before he could cross the platform, he was enthusiastically kissed by ten Frenchwomen and was barely able to stave off the embraces of twice as many Frenchmen. A group of his compatriots seized him, cheered his medal and his wound stripe, and carried him on their shoulders to the café. It was some time before Jim Thomas, still weak from his hospital sojourn, was able to beg off and leave for the veterinary hospital.

He fingered the travel orders in his tunic pocket, orders directing him to pick up a certain chestnut mare at the hospital and rejoin his regiment. Next to the orders was the letter which had reached him in the hospital from the regimental veterinary. He smiled to himself, remembering its good news that Barbara, who must have been hit when he was, was recovering from her wound. What a grand scout that old Vet was, with his stratagem of ticketing the mare as an officer's personal mount to make sure she would go back to the regiment!

Jim skirted hospital headquarters. He'd report there later, after he had found and greeted Barbara. She would be out in that fenced field. No denying it, he certainly had missed that little mare.

It was afternoon, nearing the hours for stables, when the horses in the field noticed a lone soldier in olive drab, instead of the usual detail in dungarees, walking toward them. They began to amble over, their attitude plainly saying, "Well, it was about due for somebody to remember our existence. It's time we ate."

The soldier did not open the gate but climbed up on it, shielding his eyes from the sun to stare at the horses. He whistled shrilly.

Barbara never failed to answer that summons. He watched in high anticipation for her to come galloping to him, shouldering her way through the herd. But there was no stir among them, except for the hungry horses which drifted toward him, thinking he was part of the stable detail. Probably Barbara had been kept in the hospital stables, Jim decided. Perhaps her wound was still bothering her. Best go back and ask at headquarters. That's what he should have done in the first place.

It was no easy task to pin down the hospital commandant, a jovial, red-faced major of the veterinary corps.

"Travel orders for a horse—now!" he protested. "Let it wait till tomorrow, Sergeant. Man, the war's over! I'm planning a party for my staff and can't be bothered. Join up with our noncoms, why don't you, for their celebration? They'd be glad to have you. Enough of this now. See you later."

But Jim Thomas was not to be put off, and in the end the major, out of respect for the other's empty sleeve and medal, and impressed by his earnestness, heard him out.

"Want to see that mare again, do you, soldier?" He smiled. "Well, I know how you feel. Wouldn't be a Vet if I didn't. Come on. I'll take you through the hospital. Don't know the mare myself. Only took command here a while ago. You say she's an officer's mount? That may be—on the roster—but I know whose baby she really is."

Vainly they scoured the whole hospital. Barbara simply was not there. Jim Thomas, growing desperate, faced the commandant.

"She's gone! You've lost her!" he accused angrily. "Look here, Major! What kind of an outfit is this? You can't get away with that with an officer's mount!"

"Hang it, I know it!" the other growled. "Can't see how it could have happened. Are you sure the mare was identified as an officer's mount?"

The Texan, hiding his confusion, did not answer. Of course Barbara was not a private mount and could not be actually identified as such. To substantiate it there were only the false papers furnished by his own regimental veterinary. Best not to say too much. The major, not noticing his failure to reply, talked on.

"She would have had a ticket and papers here, of course, but they've been destroyed. We had an air raid here and a fire that burned up a lot of headquarters papers. Right after that, the place was jammed with Argonne casualties. When I took over here, we had to call in inspectors and—wait! Maybe that's what happened to her."

"What?" Thomas demanded grimly.

"We had to make room," the veterinary explained. "Every horse judged likely to be permanently unfit for Army Service was condemned and sold."

"Condemned and sold!" Jim Thomas echoed him. Tragedy was written on his face, which went white and then red with wrath. "You did that to the little mare after what she's done! Why, you should have seen her bringing up the caissons at Blanc Mont! Why, you bunch of—"

"Easy, Sergeant," the officer cautioned. "How could we know? It was a rotten deal, I admit, but a mistake that couldn't be helped. Now I'll get wires busy and see what I can do. But I doubt if we've any record of where the mare went. They just auctioned off the condemned animals, fast as they could sell 'em, down in the village there. Try—"

The sergeant waited to hear no more. Through the window, the Major saw him hurrying toward the village.

They still talk sometimes in that little French town of the strange *soldat Americain* who roamed around Armistice Night asking what had become of a horse. On Armistice Night! *Quel moment!*

"*Messieurs*," they relate to visitors, "he would drink nothing! *Non, rien de tout*, though it was free! Our prettiest girls sought to distract him, for was he not handsome and a hero who had lost an arm in battle for *la belle France? Mais non encore.* He would have none of them. *Messieurs, c'est incroyable, mais c'est vrai!*"

It was the village blacksmith who gave Jim Thomas a scrap of news at last. The smith was more than half tight by that time, but he understood how strong can be a man's love for a horse.

But yes, the blacksmith declared. He had been at the auction of condemned animals sold by the Americans. And he did remember a little chestnut mare. She had caught his eye. A neat piece of horseflesh but with a bad limp of the right foreleg.

Who had bought her? The smith shrugged eloquently. How can one remember such matters when one is celebrating? *Eh, bien,* he would try to think. Was it not that farmer, a veteran disabled and discharged? The man had asked if that limp might be cured. Where dwelt the man? Around Verdun somewhere, the smith thought. He would be going back to farm there again, now the war was over.

The blacksmith waved aside Jim Thomas's thanks. It was nothing. He raised his bottle convivially. "À *la victoire, mon vieux! Aux États-Unis! À France!*"

The halt led the lame.

13: THE LONG, LONG TRAIL

My beautiful, my beautiful, that standest meekly by
With thy proudly arched and glossy neck, and dark and fiery
eye!
Fret not to roam the desert now with all thy winged speed.
I may not mount on thee again—thou'rt sold, my Arab steed!
CAROLINE NORTON: *The Arab's Farewell to His Steed*

WHEN Barbara was bought at the sale of condemned animals, her new owner took her north to the town where his family had lived as refugees since they had fled from their own home in a war area. They moved slowly, for the halt led the lame. Jean Drouet had taken a German bayonet thrust in the thigh and would gratefully have ridden his purchase. But he knew better than to risk it. This mare, for all her small size, was a bargain if she recovered from her limp. There would be much work in her, and there would be much required on his farm, once the Boche was driven back from Verdun.

So they marched by easy stages and rested often. During halts, the discharged poilu rubbed Barbara's wounded fore-quarter and leg with liniment. Before they reached their destination, he saw with satisfaction that the chestnut mare had grown slightly more limber.

His wife came out to greet him, beaming. Here was her man who, just before his horse-buying trip, had come back to her alive from the war and need not return to it because of his wound.

"See what I have bought from the Americans," he displayed. "She is little, yes. Not like our good Roland, stolen by the dirty Boche. Also she is still lame. But she was cheap—all I could afford—and she will do to work the farm when the time comes."

"May the good God grant that time comes soon!" Madame Drouet prayed. "The communiques are bright of late. The Boche retreats."

Barbara, gazing curiously about her, pricked up her ears. A girl of about ten had skipped up and stretched out a hand to pat her. This little creature with dancing brown eyes, black curls, and round, rosy cheeks was new to the mare's experience. But between them was that kinship which animals and children know, and Barbara permitted her soft nose to be stroked.

Jean Drouet smiled at his daughter. "Do not make her too much a pet, little Renée," he warned. "She is not for you. When we are home again, she must plow hard to grow us food to live."

And that became the destiny of Barbara, as of many another war horse, when the field-gray tide covering northern France ebbed at last. She was hitched to a cart— Drouet discovering with delight that she was broken to harness—but the family's meagre household goods, saved when they were evacuated, did not load it heavily. No one rode. Renée proudly led the still-limping little mare, encouraging her with endearments. Again the roads were filled with processions of refugees who four years before had traversed them in despairing flight. Now, retracing their steps, bound homeward, they were happy, though many of them were returning to houses in ruins and fields scarred with trenches and sown with steel.

Verdun! From his fields Drouet could see in the distance the citadel which the enemy had stormed vainly. They had not passed! Yet they had left their mark. There was indeed much work to be done on the farm—clearing and rebuilding—before spring planting. If Drouet had known that Arab blood flowed in Barbara's veins, that she

was a splendid jumper, it would have mattered not a whit
to him. What if she were a veteran, wounded in action?
So was he. That was all over now. Both of them must toil
to the limit of their endurance. He would spare her no
more than himself.

About the time the Drouets took the road for home,
Barbara's regiment pulled its guns out of their last em-
placements in the Argonne and began a march on the
Rhine.

Through delivered and rejoicing Belgium, through in-
different Luxembourg, they marched. On into Germany
they pressed, hard on the heels of the demoralized armies
of the vanquished. On rolled the caissons over roads lit-
tered with abandoned rifles and helmets and the gaunt,
starved bodies of dead horses. On through villages where
some watched them sullenly and others greeted them curiously, for censorship had kept not a few Germans ignorant
of the fact that the United States had entered the war. At
last the regiment halted its long hike and was billeted in a
Rhine town near the headquarters of the American zone
of occupation at Coblenz. The men in olive drab shared
their rations with the thin, flaxen-haired children. An atmosphere, hostile at first, changed to friendliness. The
war was over. Let bygones be bygones.

Alert, nevertheless, the invaders stood ready for action
till the Germans signed the fateful treaty. Still Barbara's

regiment and other Regular troops kept the watch on the Rhine, while National Army divisions sailed back across the Atlantic. Homesick but resigned to their duty, the Regulars stayed on and, proud of their name and their record, maintained the discipline which is not always easy when peace relaxes the grim insistence of warfare. The granting of leaves and the organization of entertainments and sports helped raise morale.

At the first opportunity, Captain John Brent, now a battery commander, reported to the Colonel that Sergeant Thomas had not returned, as expected, with the mare. Of course, the ticketing of Barbara as an officer's charger and the orders directing Thomas to pick her up had been devices to bring them both back to the regiment and save them from going into a replacement pool. But the devices might not have worked, or either the soldier or the mare might not have recovered from wounds. Any one of several slip-ups might have occurred, as apparently had happened.

The Colonel turned to his Adjutant. "Get after that right away," he ordered. "The war's over. It's time we were able to find out something in this man's Army. Pull any wires you have to, but get action."

It still was far from easy to trace one non-commissioned officer and one horse in the vast A.E.F., now in the turmoil of embarking divisions for home. The Adjutant, however, was a dogged, persevering fellow. Persistently he made himself obnoxious, refusing to be put off. He looked on the tape when it was red and, figuratively drawing sabre, slashed it right and left.

The first news came from the base hospital where Sergeant Thomas had been a patient. Rapidly it spread through the regiment from soldier to soldier:

"Jim Thomas got out of the hospital. . . . Pretty badly crocked up, they say. . . . They slated him for the first boat home and discharge. . . . Can yuh believe it? He puts up a kick at that. . . . He flashes orders on 'em to go and get an officer's hoss—that's Barbara—and bring her back to the outfit. . . . Sure, he don't have to obey them orders, and him all bunged up, but he makes 'em stick. . . . Seems like the surgeon there came from Texas, too, and humors him. . . . They gives him leave and lets him loose."

A report from the veterinary hospital furnished the next bulletin, circulated among all ranks:

"Say, hear what they pulled at the vet hospital where Barbara was? The double-blanked so-and-so's, they condemned and sold her! Sure, they're doing all kinds of buck-passing on it. . . . An accident, says they. . . . If any of those guys shows up around here, leave us at 'em!"

This was the next communique that filtered through from Headquarters:

"Here's the latest. . . . Jim Thomas shows up at that vet hospital. . . . He finds out what they done to Bar-

bara. . . . Can yuh hear him telling 'em off! . . .
Seems some Frog bought Barbara, but they don't know
where she's gone. . . . Jim pulls out. . . . Last seen
headed toward Verdun. . . . They don't know where he
is, either."

It was a long time before any further trace of the missing was reported. Then came this:

"Say! Jim Thomas was picked up on a road, darn near
dead of pneumonia. . . . Got him to a hospital in time
to pull him through. . . . After that they shot him
down to Nice. . . . Been there weeks getting well. . . .
Pretty soft! . . . Bet he's got some baby doll of a
nurse. . . . And us ordered not to fraternize with the
frauleins! . . . Jim's minus his left wing, but the Old
Man's fixed it for him to come back to the outfit when he's
okay."

And then came the last word the regiment was to re-
ceive for many a day.

"What do you know about this. . . . Jim's skipped
out of Nice. . . . Gone AWOL. . . . Some guys don't
know when they're well off. . . . Brent says he thinks
Jim's gone back to looking for the mare again."

The soldier trudging along the road was tired and
thirsty and covered with the white dust of Verdun.
Around here, thought Jim Thomas, it still looked as much
shot up as it had when his outfit had served in this sector.

This was still a land of shattered trees, trenches, and strands of rusty barbed wire, though it was late in the spring of 1919. They certainly had kept him a long time in the hospital and the convalescent area. Bad stuff, pneumonia, but he was fit again now.

In a truck garden beside a farmhouse, he saw a young girl weeding. Jim, thirsty, halted and touched his overseas cap.

"*Bon jour, mademoiselle.*"

"*Bon jour, m'sieu.*" The girl smiled at him.

"*Avez vous de l'eau?*"

"*Mais certainement, m'sieu. Attendez.*"

She brought him a brimming cup, her brown eyes sparkling up at him. A sweet kid.

"I speak the Eenglish," she announced proudly. "I have learn heem in the school."

"You speak it fine, too." Jim grinned.

"Sit down, *m'sieu,*" she invited. "You are *fatigué—*what you say?—tired." She glanced sympathetically at his empty sleeve. "You are wounded. My papa also."

They sat together on a bench in the sun. Jim sighed. It was a nice country, this France, but he'd seen too much of it in his futile search for Barbara. A farmer near Verdun, the blacksmith had said. Well, there were a lot of them and that covered plenty of territory. He saw no horse in the fields here. He was nearly ready to give up.

The child was chattering on, enjoying practicing her

English. He, she told him, was the first American soldier she had met, and such a nice one. An older friend of hers named Marie used to write to one because she was his *marraine de guerre.*

"His what?" asked Jim Thomas.

"His godmother of the war," the girl explained. "Many French girl adopt a soldier to write and cheer heem when he is at the Front. *Hélas!* Now the war eet is over and I—"

"Weren't you anybody's *marraine?*" Jim broke in.

The girl sadly shook her head.

"Reckon it's not too late," said the gallant Texan. "Will you be mine?" He grinned, thinking how like an old-fashioned proposal that sounded.

"Oh, *m'sieu!*" she cried. "How I am overjoyed! Yes, I weel be yours," she promised sweetly. *"Ta marriane de guerre."*

"My name's Jim," he said. "You'll write me, won't you?"

"But yes! I have lovely paper for writing and the pretty purple ink." She bubbled on like a brook. "I shall my letters commence, '*Mon cher filleul*—My dear godson! I shall write to you of many things—of the dear little horse I love—"

"Horse?" Jim demanded. "Where?"

"In the field behind the house, plowing with papa. I—"

"Come on. Let's see. What's your name?"

"Renée, *m'sieu*." She trustingly gave him her hand and they hurried around the house into the field.

Barbara saw her Jim first. She halted in a furrow and neighed a joyous, poignant welcome.

It was their happiest reunion. The feet of both of them had been set on a long, long trail leading to a land where faith alone tells a mortal that he may meet his loved ones again—kinsfolk and friends and loyal animals. They had turned back and at long last found each other. Jim Thomas fondled the mare, rubbing the scar on her shoulder. Barbara, questioning and fond, nosed his empty sleeve. How shaggy she was! How tired she looked! This grand little mare pulling a plow! She was not made for that. It would end by killing her. The Texan began talking volubly.

While the dumbfounded Drouet leaned on his plow handles and gaped, Renée interpreted as best she could, half delighted, half dismayed.

"So? She was once yours?" Drouet said. "Yet she is mine now. I bought her and I paid for her."

"You've got to give her back!" Jim Thomas declared.

"I must?" snapped the ex-poilu. "Who says I must?" Then and there, Verdun was close to seeing a post-war battle.

"Oh, I'll give you what you paid for her and more," the American offered. He pulled out a prodigious roll of francs, back pay he had not had the opportunity—or inclination—to spend.

It was their happiest reunion

Drouet, mollified, accepted a handsome bid and, un-hitching Barbara, they went back to the house where a bill of sale was made out. The farmer closed the deal happily. Now he could buy a strong work horse.

Ready to lead Barbara away, Jim saw a pathetic little figure by the wall, sobbing as if her heart would break.

"Oh, Renée, I'm awful sorry. I forgot you love her, too," he said contritely. He knelt down and put his arm around her. On the other side, Barbara gently nuzzled the girl's neck.

"But you have love her first, and she loves you," the child smiled bravely. "Eet is best she go with you and not work so hard here. Take her, *m'sieu*. She is yours."

"I'll write you about her—always," Jim promised. "And some day maybe we'll come to see you." He rose to go. He couldn't stand any more of this.

"*Au revoir*, my little *marraine*," he called back.

Her soft voice followed him.

"*Au revoir, mon cher filleul*."

never was such a homecoming

14: THE REGIMENT'S OWN

For me the crossed cannons—
They never will run—
The limber and rolling caisson,
The trace and the collar,
The rumble of gun,
As we follow the Red Guidon.
COL. GERALD E. GRIFFIN: *The Red Guidon*

THE tumult and the shouting from the little German
town in the regiment's area drifted up to Headquarters.

It swelled louder and louder. The Officer of the Guard turned deadly pale and leaped into action.

"The Krauts have busted loose again!" he yelled. "Maybe it's even Black Jack Pershing on an inspection tour! Turn out the guard! Call the Colonel! Where's that darn bugler? Sound the Call to Arms!"

Billets boiled over with running soldiers. The horses on the picket lines snorted and kicked. In spite of the rush and confusion, the well-disciplined organization was rapidly preparing itself for any emergency when it was discovered that the uproar in town had resolved into a riotously noisy but peacably inclined parade bound for camp.

At the end of the cheering, cavorting khaki throng rode Sergeant Jim Thomas on the chestnut mare. The soldier was obviously pleased, though painfully embarrassed. But Barbara was eating it up. She stepped high and tossed her head right and left. She was the Queen of the May. She was an actress taking a curtain call. She was a great lady receiving homage due.

Never was there such a homecoming. The parade came to a halt before the smiling Colonel, the regiment's former second in command. Jim Thomas, redder than ever, swung from the saddle and saluted smartly with his good right arm.

"Sir, Sergeant Thomas, Batt'ry D, reports with the mare, as ordered."

The staff welcomed him, shaking his hand all around. The Colonel gave him assurance that it would be managed somehow to keep him on duty with the regiment, one-armed though he was. Jim spent the rest of the day telling his story and trying to keep Barbara from being made sick by admirers who had raided the mess halls for sugar. The evening demanded no less strenuous efforts from him to keep his head above a sea of German beer.

A week later Thomas received instructions.

" 'Tis the Colonel's orders," Stable Sergeant Michael Quinn informed him, "that you're to inter the mare in the regimental horse show. I'm not asking if you can ride her, and you minus a wing, for I know you can."

"I reckon," said the other quietly.

"Thin start schooling the mare. She'll nade it, and she after pulling a plow."

"*Bueno*," the Texan agreed. "I'll get her in shape. You'll see she can outjump anything in the outfit."

Captain Brent walked up. "Got our horse show team fixed up, Sergeant Quinn?" he inquired.

"Yis, sor. We've as good as won."

"Wait a bit now," the officer interposed. "There's a rub. You must realize that Barbara isn't a battery horse any longer. She was regularly condemned and sold out of the service. Sergeant Thomas here bought her back with his own money. She's his private property. As such she's got no place on our strength and can't be carried on the forage returns. Not that that makes a darn bit of difference. The battery fund will take care of her. But as private property of an enlisted man she can't jump in the show."

The two sergeants looked nonplussed.

"I forgot about that, sir," Jim Thomas admitted. "But, look here. Why can't I sell her back? It's not the money I care about, of course. But I'd like to have her do her bit for the honor of the battery—and she'd like to, too. And she might be safer that way than belonging to me. Could the Captain fix it?"

"It'll take some wangling, but I think I can," said Brent. And he did manage to put it through.

Barbara, as Jim promised, could and did outjump anything in the outfit. Furthermore, she could and would and did outjump anything in the division. Her quiet-mannered master strove hard not to show his pride. There were other worlds to conquer. The grapevine had it that a corps horse show would be scheduled, and a corps comprised many mounted organizations, including cavalry, which would furnish stiff competition. Thomas, relieved of most of his other duties, trained the mare carefully, calling up the lore he had learned in the days when he had worked with thoroughbreds in Kentucky.

For him the time sped by quickly. He did not feel the restlessness which gripped his comrades who, during the war, had lived only from day to day, but now, experiencing the inevitable reaction, were eager only to get home. He, Jim Thomas, with no close ties to urge him homeward, had much to look forward to right here in Germany. He had trained and loved a score of horses and had taken pride in their achievements in round-ups, on polo fields, and in jumping events. But he and Barbara had passed through a great adventure together. She had come closer to his heart than any of the others. Her triumph would seem sweetest of all.

The little mare was a natural jumper. Unridden, she cleared broomsticks, held shoulder high, with the grace and rhythm of a wild thing. However, as Thomas well knew, jumping with a man up was a different matter. Then it became a duet—at its best a perfect collaboration between rider and horse. He taught Barbara not to rush her fences but to approach them at a steady gallop, facing them squarely, never at an angle. Riding forward, he would gather her for the leap with gentle pressure of bit and heels, yet always allow her to decide when to take off.

Steadily exercised, groomed to a fare-thee-well (every driver in the battery would have rubbed her down in relays if Thomas had allowed it), Barbara was in splendid condition. Thomas himself even went into training over the protest of Sergeant Quinn.

"Here you are in a country where the best beer in the world do be flowing," the stable sergeant pointed out. "Not to mention some liquid high explosive called *schnapps*. And you pass it up."

"I've seen too many riders go into the ring liquored up," Thomas declared. "Some of them won, but it wasn't their fault. Their horses did it in spite of 'em."

"Well, 'tis for the honor iv the rigimint," Quinn conceded. " 'Tis worth the sacryfice it is."

When the corps horse show opened, and event after event was run off, the honor of the regiment seemed bound to fare well. A mixed section from the regiment won the mounted drill competition. A major, who had joined during the latter part of the regiment's active service, took third with one of his two personal mounts in the officers' jumping class. The enlisted men's jumping class followed. It was for this event that everyone in the outfit not on duty—and some who were supposed to be—had come.

They crowded around the ring to watch the eliminations. Barbara, jumping like a deer, never faltered. At every trial she turned in a perfect performance. At last three horses remained: the chestnut mare; a fine, lithe bay ridden by a cavalryman; and a strong roan, with an artilleryman from another division up.

The roan's rider, in his excitement, began "riding on his reins." There is a saying among horsemen that the heaviest thing on the back of a horse is the hands of the rider. So it proved now, but the roan—doughty animal! —carried on, though his form suffered. He matched the bay and the chestnut on the first round. The three judges in the ring motioned for another rail to be added, putting the jump up to four feet.

It was then the Colonel of the regiment saw an officer of his rank enter the stands and made room on the seat beside him. Recognition dawned. The newcomer was he who had briefly commanded the regiment, the martinet who had attempted to take Barbara for his own mount. They greeted each other with coolness.

"I hear your outfit has an entry still in. Which one?" inquired the harsh voice of the late arrival.

"The chestnut mare there," was the short answer.

The other stared. "Say, that's the stumbler!" he exclaimed.

"The same. But she's improved. The sergeant insists she can make the jumps."

"Humph. Once a stumbler always a stumbler. My bet's the bay. Care to risk a thousand francs on your nag, Colonel?"

"Certainly, Colonel. Done."

"Done. It's easy money for me or somebody was a liar,"

came the gruff rejoinder. "That chestnut's due for a smashup."

But it was the roan that crashed. His head was held in by his rider when the horse was put to the fence. It was like tying a man's arms behind him and expecting him to take a high hurdle. The roan made a gallant effort, failed to rise enough and lit on the fence like a ton of bricks.

Now it was the bay's turn. The cavalry horse rose to the fence handsomely but tipped with one fore-hoof. In the crowd around the ring the men of the regiment could not contain themselves. Maybe it was unsportsmanlike to cheer an opponent's failure, yet they could not resist.

"Yah!" they yelled. "Who won the war? The cavalry!"

Muttering cavalrymen clenched their fists. Hard-boiled military police pushed into the crowd to stave off a riot.

Barbara had only to clear four feet, a height she had managed often before. Jim Thomas rode her slowly by the fence, as if to let her measure it with her eyes. Then he turned her and launched her at it. Up and over she soared.

Alas! One hind hoof lightly tipped the top bar.

"Yah!" roared the cavalrymen. "Who won the war? The wagon soldiers! Take that plug back and hitch it to a caisson!"

The M.P.'s had a tough time keeping order. The Commanding General signaled to his bugler to blow "Attention." Only then was calm restored.

Back came the bay and the chestnut for the jump-off. What splendid animals they were! Beautifully, gracefully, they both took the jumps without a tip. Barbara cleared them with a full foot to spare. It was her victory, the cheers seemed to say.

But the judges were undecided. Both horses had accomplished a faultless performance. The decision must rest on an inspection of their riders. They called over the cavalry sergeant and Thomas. The two fine-appearing soldiers stood to attention. Nothing could be found wrong in their bearing, uniforms or equipment. At last the judges were reduced to looking for identification tags, the two metal discs which a soldier is supposed to wear on a tape around his neck. The cavalryman had forgotten his entirely. Sergeant Thomas's, while they were not in their proper place, were at least on his person—on a key ring in his pocket.

The judges pinned a blue ribbon on Barbara. Up in the stands, a Colonel, with a snarl and an exceedingly dirty look, paid a thousand-franc loss.

Captain John Brent sought out Thomas and the mare at the stable.

"Congratulations to the two of you," he said warmly. "I couldn't be more delighted."

"I'd rather hear that from the Captain than from anybody else, sir," Thomas answered. "Barbara was

"Who won the war? Cavalry!"

"Who won the war? C'mon boy."

your horse. You could have been riding her today."

"Not so well as you rode her. I've never regretted letting you have her."

"Some'll be saying we won by a couple of dog tags," the sergeant remarked with a smile. "But Barbara outjumped that bay."

"She sure did. By the way, Sergeant, which did you take—the week's leave or the money prize?"

"Took the two hundred francs, sir. I reckoned I might need it somehow."

"And maybe you didn't want to go off and leave the mare in care of somebody else?" Brent put in, grinning.

"The boys would take good care of her," Thomas said, grinning back an acknowledgment.

Brent's expression sobered. "Sergeant, I suppose you're prepared, you've got yourself all set for the day—the day when—"

"What day, sir?"

"The day when we go home and—and—have to turn in our horses."

"*Turn in our horses!*" The sergeant's face paled under its tan. "Why *we* don't do that! That's just the National Army outfits. They're going to be mustered out. We're Regulars. Our regiment'll stay in the service. It'll need its horses."

"Right. But there's lots of horses in the States. Orders

are that we dispose of the ones we have here. Got to leave them in Europe. There's no cargo space for them and won't be for many months."

The Texan's eyes flashed. "That seems like the lowest, orneriest trick I ever heard of! Didn't they fight the war with us! And now we go and hand 'em over to the butcher!"

"No, not that. They won't be destroyed—none of them that's fit. They'll be sold to the French and Belgian and Polish armies. Some of them to French and German civilians."

Thomas laid a hand protectively on Barbara's mane. "No man," he announced grimly, "is going to take this little mare away from me—not into the kind of hell she got when she was with that French outfit."

"Steady, man," the captain warned. "You can't buck the Army. You can't smuggle the mare aboard ship the way B Battery did its mascot dog coming over. I've been thinking about this problem ever since I knew about the orders. And I'm not the only one. It's been talked over at the officers' mess often. Barbara's got good friends in the outfit."

"I know she has, sir."

"Our first hunch was for one of us to take her back as a personal mount."

"That'll do it, sir. I'd trust her to an officer of this outfit

—one of the ones really fond of horses. They'd always take good care of her."

"Trouble is it can't be done, Sergeant. The strict ruling is that any officer who brought over a personal mount— and we've got a few who did, as you know,—is entitled to take it back with him. If an officer didn't bring a horse of his own to France, there's absolutely nothing doing on taking one back. The Colonel tried to do some wire pulling and got nowhere. We let you in for this trouble, getting you to sell her so she could be in this show. Barbara's a public animal now. She belongs to the U.S.A.—on the record. She'll have to be sold at auction."

"I'll be hanged if—"

"Hold on now. I've got another plan. You take your prize money—some more of us friends of Barbara's will chip in—and we'll get some German civilian, some kind-hearted Kraut who'll be good to her, to buy her in. Maybe next year we can get her shipped back home."

Thomas looked into the distance. "There's going to be trouble in this country after we leave," he predicted. "But any man who loved horses, Heine or not, would be good to Barbara. Reckon that's the best that can be done, sir. Thanks a lot."

"I'll get the money," Brent promised. "All the officers from the Colonel down want to chip in."

"Thanks again, sir, but would you hold off a while?"

Thomas asked. "I hear there's another big horse show on —one for the whole Army of Occupation. Maybe Barbara and me can go and catch us another prize."

He stroked the mare's forehead gently, while her soft eyes rested on him.

"Barbara and me," he hesitated—"Barbara and me would kinda like to try and earn that money ourselves."

She soared,
poised over the top bar.

15: HEART OVER A FENCE

> Gently Roushan Beg caressed
> Kyrat's forehead, neck, and breast;
>   Kissed him upon both his eyes,
> Sang to him in his wild way,
> As upon the topmost spray
>   Sings a bird before it flies. . . .

Kyrat, then, the strong and fleet,
Drew together his four white feet,
Paused a moment on the verge,
Measured with his eye the space,
And into the air's embrace
Leaped as leaps the ocean surge.
LONGFELLOW: *The Leap of Roushan Beg*

IT was the final afternoon of the carnival of sports, staged by the American Army of Occupation. Blue and gold in the sun, the waters of the Rhine swirled around the island, just above Coblenz, where the walls of the new stadium rose. Ten stables housing the seven hundred horses taking part in the show flanked the great structure. Emerging from one of them, Stable Sergeant Michael Quinn walked toward the stadium, where he was hailed by Captain John Brent, waiting for him in an entrance.

"Sergeant," Brent said, returning a salute, "I sort of thought you and I ought to watch this last big event together. After all, you and I knew Barbara from the first. You might say we stood as her godfathers."

"We did that, sor. Is the Captain sure he wouldn't rather sit in the officers' stand?"

"Positive. We'll stand by the barrier opposite the middle jump. You've just come from the stable, haven't you? How's the mare?"

"A bit tired, sor, I'd say. But she'll do."

"No wonder she's tired. Man, she's done magnificently! When you and Thomas won the pair jumping yesterday, Barbara and that sorrel of yours went over every jump in perfect step. And this morning Barbara plain ran away with the enlisted men's jumping class."

"But now it's the open, sor. Champeenship of the A. of O., they say. The mare'll be jumping against officers' mounts—thoroughbreds and the like."

"Sure, but she'll come through. Thomas all right? Nervous?"

"Not that lad. If he is, he don't show it, sor."

"Good. Come along, Sergeant."

Placing himself on the left and slightly to the rear, Sergeant Quinn accompanied his officer in a military manner.

Within the arena, decorated with evergreen boughs and arches bound with bright-colored bunting, bands were playing. Its rising tiers were black with many thousands of spectators. From the central box opposite the bandstand, the American Secretary of War watched, his dark, keen face alive with interest. On his right sat Belgian royalty and on his left the straight, soldierly figure of General Pershing, strong jaw square-set under trim, gray mustache, eagle eyes sweeping the arena's olive drab expanse—men he had led through a great war. Behind him and around him sat more generals—French, British, American.

"Gosh! Look at them generals!" murmured a dough-boy, glancing up at the box. "This ain't no place to try to get away with somethin'."

There was a commotion, then a hush. Contestants in the open jumping class were riding into the ring—officers, in rank from colonel to captain, on strong, splendid mounts whose glossy coats glistened in the bright light. Brent's and Quinn's hearts sank as they watched them from the barrier. Last—a little late—entered a sergeant of artillery on a small chestnut mare.

The regiment was up first, madly cheering its own. The division was on its feet, too, claiming them and acclaiming them. There was no field artilleryman in the stadium who did not rasp his throat raw, nor any soldier of any arm of the service who did not cheer them to an echo. The story of these two entering the ring had spread through the Army of Occupation. Gallant horse and gallant rider, with his empty left sleeve pinned to the breast of his tunic! The tumult surged and sank and surged again, like great breakers thundering on a rocky shore, as men who felt a lump in their throats and moisture in the corners of their eyes gulped, winked and cheered themselves hoarse again.

Over in the bandstand the leader made frantic motions with his baton. Out rang the familiar strains of *The Caisson Song*.

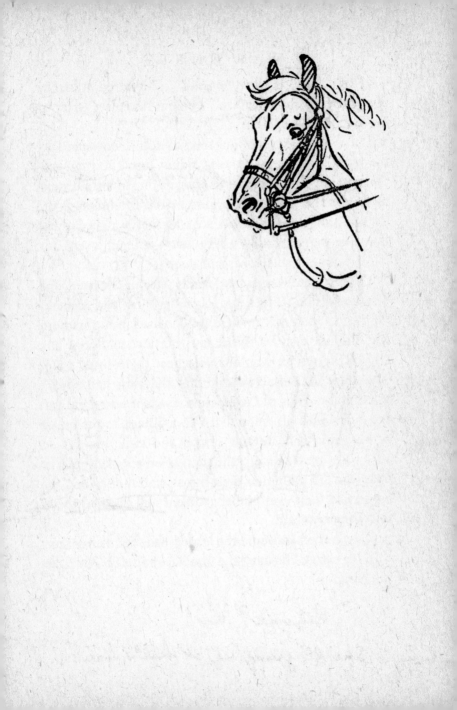

"Refuse? no!
She'll jump if it kills her."

Paul Brown

Over hill, over dale,
We have hit the dusty trail,
And those caissons go rolling along. . . .

Up went Barbara's ears. She stepped along in time, like the veteran she was, while Thomas, swallowing hard, sat her straight and proudly.

One of the judges in the stand turned to another.

"That little chestnut mare," he indicated. "Is it true she has no breeding?"

"Yes. She's not in the book," came the answer. "They claim in her regiment she came off a range out West. But she's got blood in her from somewhere."

"Right you are. She's done marvelously in the show so far. But she's out of her class now."

Orderlies had arranged six fences on the circuit, with the bars at three and one-half feet. Every entry breezed around without difficulty, although superiorities of form were noted. Up went the bars to three-feet-nine. Now horses began to drop, ruled out for tipping, for knocking down the top bar or for refusals. At four feet, a stiff course, the casualties came thick and fast.

Then it was that the regiment's new major was eliminated. After making five leaps handsomely, he dropped the timber on the sixth. Smiling like the sportsman he was, he rode past Sergeant Thomas.

"Heah's wishing you luck, Sergeant," he said in his

soft Virginia speech. "Reckon it's up to you to carry through for the regiment. Might have done betteh on my otheh horse, but he's undeh the weatheh. Couldn't beat that mare of yours anyhow. Best luck."

"Thanks, sir."

Over the bars at 4.3—at 4.6—at 4.9 soared the beautiful little chestnut, while her competitors dwindled fast. The stands were heaving, uproarious waves of olive drab, with a spray of overseas caps flung high in the air. The dignified Secretary of War was observed barely to have restrained himself at the last moment from slapping Belgian royalty on the back.

A Colonel of Polish Cavalry, sitting next to the Colonel of Barbara's regiment, exploded with a string of consonants from which a few words of broken English finally filtered: "That mare—I buy her—much money!"

"Not for sale—not if I can help it," the American emphatically assured him. Down by the barrier, Captain Brent and Sergeant Quinn were yelling, jumping up and down and pumping each other's hands in a highly undisciplined fashion.

The judges ordered the bars of that last fence put up to five feet. Only two horses were now in the running: Barbara and a magnificent black thoroughbred, ridden by a young captain of cavalry.

Jim Thomas, dismounted, waited while his opponent

rode out into the course. How tired the little mare was! She was breathing hard and her coat was sweat-streaked. He'd been a fool, Thomas moaned, to ride her this morning, yet he never had believed she had a chance in the Open this afternoon. Contritely, he patted her on the neck. Barbara turned as she always did when he patted her and gave him a look, just such a tender look, Thomas told himself, as a woman who loved you might bestow.

"I know, old girl, I know," he answered her. "Tired as you are, you won't let me and the regiment down."

The black thoroughbred, expertly ridden, was doing his blue blood proud. Over the first five jumps he sailed, galloped hard for the five-footer and drew an arc over it like a howitzer trajectory. Tumultuous cheering rewarded the fine performance.

Brent and Quinn saw Thomas stroke the mare's forehead and whisper something into an ear. He mounted up, rode to the head of the course. Barbara stepped out springily, head up, all her fatigue appearing to have melted away. They halted at the line.

"Now," said the rider softly, and the mare leaped forward.

Rat-tat-tat, rat-tat-tat, drummed her hoofs in the deep silence. A sudden hush in the miniature thunder, as she took off for the first jump. Then that flight through the air which, for a true horseman, no plane can surpass.

Rat-tat, rat-tat—fore and hind feet alighting. Once again the stirring staccato of the gallop.

Two—three—four—five—fences. She was over them all. Ahead, seeming like a mountain, loomed the last high jump.

She looked so small, the little mare, approaching that towering obstacle. Surely it was too much for her, too much for her valiant, faithful spirit. Not a man of all those thousands in the stands but sat breathless on the edge of his seat and with all the strength of his will prepared to help lift her over that jump.

Most of all, the man on her back gave her every ounce of the strength of his will power and his love for her. If you throw your heart over a fence, they say, your horse will follow it. And Jim Thomas, in those fleeting seconds, threw his.

The tattoo of hoofs rose to a crescendo—ceased. The mare sprang forward. Neck far outstretched, forelegs doubled, haunches gathered under her, mane and tail flowing, she soared, poised over the top bar a fleeting instant for a glimpse which portrayed the purest poetry of motion. Then, gliding down, she alighted with infinite grace and galloped on.

Jim Thomas never heard the tremendous outburst of cheers that rocked the stadium as he rode to the judges' stand. He dreaded too much what he expected to hear there, and hear it he did.

"There'll have to be a jump-off," was the ruling. "Raise the bar on the last fence to 5.3."

Barbara, her flanks heaving, was trembling in every limb. The cavalry captain turned his big black toward the course, but Thomas swung out of his saddle and addressed the senior judge.

"Sorry, sir," he said. "Count me out."

"That gives the championship to the black," the officer warned. "Think your mare is likely to refuse this time?"

"No, sir, not her," Thomas flashed back. "She'll jump if it kills her. But she's done in, and I'm not going to ask it of her."

They pinned the blue ribbon on the black's bridle, the red on Barbara. Saluting and congratulating the winner, Thomas led the mare from the arena.

Rubbing her down in the stable, the sergeant heard footsteps. He and Barbara looked back to see a circle of familiar faces. General Mack, now commanding the brigade, was there, with the Colonel, the Adjutant, Captain Carrick, Brent, First Sergeant McNally, and Quinn.

"Sorry we couldn't bring it off, sir," Jim Thomas said to the Colonel.

"Wouldn't have had you do otherwise than you did, Sergeant," that officer answered cordially. "We're all right proud of you both."

"Have to try somehow to take this mascot of the regiment back home with us," General Mack put in. "It won't be long now before we leave. I can't deny we'll face plenty of trouble trying to take the mare along. I might chance taking it up with General Pershing. He's an old cavalryman and loves horses, but he's a stickler for orders, too."

"If the mare has to go up at auction, I know a Polish Colonel who'll bid his head off to get her," the regiment's commander declared.

The circle relapsed into gloomy silence. Thomas, his face hard, rubbed Barbara's slender legs with straw.

"Beg pardon, gentlemen. That was mighty fine jumping today."

It was the major from Virginia who had joined them. Except for an abstracted nod or two, none of the melancholy group around the stall paid any attention.

"Mighty fine jumping," the major repeated. Still he was ignored. How could he, a newcomer to the regiment, they reflected, understand the sadness filling the hearts of these men who had known Barbara for so long? What did it matter how well she had jumped, if they must go home without her?

"I've just had some bad news," the major persisted.

That drew a polite murmur. His auditors, too, dreaded some of the same—an order from the Remount which would mean the loss of this old friend of theirs.

But the major insisted on being heard. "Just had word

my otheh horse—the one I couldn't ride today—has glanders. Has to be destroyed. Now I brought two personal mounts oveh heah and I'm entitled to take back two. I reckoned I might—if you-all agree—take this little mare heah back as my second mount."

That was how Barbara sailed back home with her regiment.

I'm her image

16: TALE OF TWO VETERANS

Hail and farewell, old horse, to you
Our comrade of the Russian Ride,
Night march, maneuver and review,
And of the polo field beside.
Our pet, our pest, and yet our pride
Much of our heart goes with you still
As with the Eighteenth Field astride
You take the last long road to Sill.

WAR HORSE

From Rhine to Rio Grande, we two
Have taken battle in our stride.
The prairie sun, the ocean blue,
Have tanned and toughened up our hide,
Hunger and fear and wounds have tried
All of our courage and our will.
We lose a comrade from our side—
You take the last long road to Sill.

At Fort Sam Houston you're all through—
Motors don't wait for time or tide;
And as you slowly pass from view
We crank 'em up and let 'em slide.
But with this thought we're satisfied—
Elysian fields lie o'er the hill
To horse and buggy days it's tied.
So take the last long road to Sill.

Envoy
Old Horse—the Gods can still provide
Polo, and hunts, and mounted drill.
You'll be as welcome as a bride;
So take the last long road to Sill.

COL. JOHN N. GREELY: *Ballade*

THROUGH the Texas city of San Antonio, past the historic Alamo, a rancher rode. His chestnut mare was old —close to her thirties—but she was trim and light-footed still. The man astride her expertly rolled a cigarette with one hand (he lacked a left arm), lit it with *briquette* and blew the smoke between his mount's ears. She flicked them playfully back at him. Between these two was an old comradeship, one of more than a score of years now.

Beyond the city the Stars and Stripes, fluttering from a tall staff, marked the Army post of Fort Sam Houston. The mare, catching sight of it, quickened her pace, and her rider's gray eyes brightened. They passed through the gate and headed for the artillery barracks. A gap between buildings gave a glimpse of troops forming on the parade ground.

Suddenly the horseman swung his steed across the path of a soldier hurrying, head down, toward the gate.

"Hold up there, Mike Quinn," he called, dismounting. "What's your hurry?"

The sergeant halted and looked up.

"Jim Thomas and Barbara, the daughter iv the rigimint, no liss!" he greeted. "You old-timers was due to be paying us a visit agin. You ain't dropped over for a year."

"Been busy on the ranch," Jim explained. "First chance Barbara and me had to take a *pasear* over here and see old friends."

"How's the missus?" Quinn inquired.

"Renée's fine," said Jim, "and so's the kids."

"Renée ain't got tired iv an ould feller like you?"

Jim grinned. "Seems not."

"Sure and she must still be feeling flattered by you waiting eight years for her to grow up and going back to France to marry her. She may nivver git over being plazed and surprised. That's your wan chanst."

Barbara stamped a forefoot and moved her head in between the two men.

Thomas laughed. "Mike, she don't like being left out of a conversation. I swear she understands a lot of talk."

Quinn patted the mare's neck and spoke to her. " 'Tis rude I was, niglicting you, ould dear. And how are you?"

Her master answered for her. "She's fine. We ride the range together still—pretty near as good as ever. She don't need a bridle. My voice and knees are enough, and I've got my arm free for roping."

Quinn faced the mare again. "Barbara, how's thim rip-snorting stallions you was kaping company with back in your younger days?"

Barbara turned her head aside with matronly dignity.

"They've gone out of her life," Thomas grinned. "But she's fond of her offsprings. She's counting on seeing now that filly of hers I gave Major Brent. Renée rides her other filly. That filly's colts, Barbara's grandsons, belong to our kids. It's all in the family."

Bugles were blowing the "Assembly." Quinn hastily turned toward the gate again.

"I ain't standing that formation," he said. "I'm off to town."

"What's wrong? Need a drink?"

"Nivver more thin now. You ain't heard the news. We're losing our horses forivver. The rigimint's been motorized." He shook his head sadly.

"Great guns, no!" Jim Thomas was plainly shocked.

"Yep," Quinn groaned. " 'Tis truck-drawn we'll be from this day on. We'll be feeding and watering at gas stations—when iny is convanient. We'll be picketing at tourist camps. We'll go into action—if we can foind parking space. If the inemy shows a red light, we'll stop dead. Wurra, wurra! I hope we breaks down, and little boys hollers at us, 'Git a horse!' "

"Reckon it had to come," Thomas said sadly. "But there'll still be some horsed field artillery in the Army, won't there? There's country where trucks and tractors can't go."

"Our nags goes to some of thim outfits at Fort Sill and ilsewhere," Quinn confirmed. "They'll still be horsed. 'Tis some consylation, but the boys here is broken up. Lots of the drivers had their pitchers took with their pairs. The Colonel has been prisinted with a framed photygraph iv the heads iv all the ould horses. He says the rigimintal toast is now going to be, 'Stand to heel, min!' 'Bye, Jim," he called, leaving. "I'm off to drink that toast."

"So long, Mike. I'll be seeing you some time."

Thomas rode toward the parade ground. He reined in by the side of a barrack where his presence would not be noticed.

"And the caissons go rolling along"

"We don't want to be seen, Barbara," he told the mare. "Might make the boys feel worse. I know how they feel from those times I lost you."

Side by side, the man and the mare stood quietly watching.

Officers and men of the regiment were formed along both sides of the route of departure, paying their last respects, saying farewell. Down that long avenue wound the horse column—teams with guns and caissons and led pairs. The khaki ranks doing them honor stood at rigid attention.

Bands crashed into *The Caisson Song.*

> *Over hill, over dale,*
> *We will hit the dusty trail. . . .*

Jim Thomas and Barbara drank in the well-loved strains to their close. Now the last of the column was clearing the Post. Again the bands struck up and poured forth the poignant chords of *Auld Lang Syne.*

Jim gulped as hard as he knew his old comrades out there were doing. He put an affectionate arm around the mare's neck, then climbed into the saddle.

"Come on, Barbara, old girl," he said. "That's all we can take. We've still got each other. Let's be going along."

WAR HORSE

The mare stood, as if waiting for something.

Out on the parade, the new rubber-tired guns of the regiment thundered in salute to the vanishing column.

The old war horse snorted and pawed the earth. Through the drifting smoke, she turned homeward.